Brace for Impact

A Cliff Knowles Mystery
By Russell Atkinson

Dedication

For Miles

Chapter 1

Now – Friday afternoon

The first sensation was sound. It was a familiar sound, but for a second he couldn't place it. Then the second sensation hit him in a wave – smell. Smoke! The sound was fire and he could feel the warmth of it now. He was surrounded by fire. He opened his eyes but they were immediately assaulted by the acrid sting of smoke. Tears flowed in protection, obscuring his vision. Where was he? What was happening? He tried to rise, but couldn't.

A feeling of panic rose in his throat. He began to cough. What was holding him down? He couldn't see, so he began to feel. His hands found the answer: his seat belt. His memory began to come back. He was flying back to the Bay Area with Jim Crosby. They must have crashed. They were on the ground and on fire. He had to get out. He unbuckled the belt and climbed out of the wreckage.

The ground was uneven and rocky. It was so steep he nearly fell. He couldn't see much besides a blur, so he picked his way carefully step-by-step away from the wreckage, away from the fire. As soon as he got clear he checked himself over. He decided he was unscathed, remarkably so. He turned back toward the plane and wiped his eyes. He could make out a few things. The plane was relatively intact, the fuselage, at least, although the tail section was separated from the main body. Both wings had been sheared off and lay at the foot of a blackened tree skeleton. That tree must have broken their fall to some extent. Jim was a superb pilot and must have aimed for the tree. He'd saved their lives.

Their lives! Where was Jim? He must still be in the plane! He rushed back toward the fuselage, shielding his face from the flames with one arm. The cabin was filled with dense smoke but a man's form could still be seen in the pilot's seat. Then he saw it – a tree limb protruding through the windshield – and through the pilot. Jim, a fellow retired agent, had been skewered and was roasting like shish kebab. The fire was too intense to get any closer and there was obviously nothing he could do to save him. He backed away and sat down. He had to think.

For the first time, he really surveyed his surroundings. He was in a narrow ravine with sheer rock walls on both sides. The foliage was mostly scrub with a few small trees confined to the creek area at the bottom. This must be somewhere in the Sierras. He needed to think about survival. He suddenly realized he wasn't wearing his glasses. No wonder he couldn't see well. They must have come off in the crash. He'd been wearing prescription sunglasses in the plane.

He felt his pockets. No glasses, no phone. Think, man, think!

The tail section of the plane had broken off. It was close to the fire, but not in flames. He remembered Jim telling him to put his suitcase in the back. There was other equipment and Jim's bag there as well. He rose and spotted the blood on his pants. He pulled up his pant leg and saw the gash. It hadn't hurt until now. It still didn't, but it looked like it had bled pretty heavily. It had mostly crusted over, but there was still a regular seepage trickling down his ankle.

He didn't have time to think about that now. He had to get the stuff out of the tail section before it caught fire. He made his way to the wreckage and crawled into the crumpled form. He pulled out both suitcases. There was a first aid kit in there, too. He went back in and found it attached to the side. He pulled it free and took it out along with a space blanket that was kept there. The only other item in the section was a small case, too small to be luggage.

He grabbed it and yanked it free, then rolled away. The flames were creeping closer and his legs protested the searing heat in no uncertain terms. He stood and moved his hoard farther from the plane. He watched the fire insinuate itself into the tail section.

The pile at his feet was it, the whole shebang. There was nothing more to be salvaged. He could only hope there was a working phone somewhere it there. He opened the smaller case. Inside was a gun, specifically a Sig Sauer semi-automatic 9mm pistol. He knew immediately it had been Jim's Bureau gun. When agents retire, the FBI gives them the option of purchasing their guns. Jim had obviously exercised that option. A quick check established that the gun was unloaded, but there were two fully loaded magazines and a box of ammo in the case.

He didn't think he'd need the gun, but it might come in handy if he needed to shoot something for food. There was no holster, at least not in the case. He'd examine Jim's bag for that at some point, but he had priorities right now. He had to stop the bleeding and he had to call for help.

He opened his own suitcase and sat down. He'd only expected to be away overnight, so there wasn't a lot in it, clothes mostly. He pulled out a necktie. He was still dressed in his suit, but he had taken off his tie and shoved it into his bag when he'd gotten to the airport. He opened the first aid kit from the plane, squirted some antibacterial cream on a gauze pad, placed it on the gash, then tied the necktie around it. Then he noticed a cell phone in the kit. That surprised him. It was a good idea, he supposed. What could be more helpful in case of an injury or sickness than a way to contact emergency services? But how could Jim keep it charged?

He pressed the power button and the screen came to life. Jim must have charged it within the last day. The battery icon showed it had over a quarter of its juice left. He tried to access the home screen but the phone asked for a PIN. He didn't have the PIN, but he knew that the law required any phone to have a way to call 911 without a PIN. Sure enough, there was an icon on the lock screen for emergency. He pressed it. The phone responded with a no service message. In this narrow ravine there would be no cell coverage, but they were probably too far from any cell tower anyway. When he got near civilization, he now had a way to summon help. He turned the phone off to save the battery and stashed it in his pocket.

A thorough search of both bags proved that there was no cell phone in Jim's bag, but his own phone was there. He'd turned it off and stashed it there before the flight since the battery was dead. He hadn't charged it overnight at the hotel because he'd forgotten his charging cord. No matter. He had the emergency phone from the first aid kit. Just as important for now: his regular glasses were in his suitcase. He put them on. Somehow the new visual clarity allowed him to think. It was his prescription sunglasses that he had lost in the crash.

Water. The thought struck him that people stranded in the mountains, the ones who die, usually die from thirst. The very thought made him suddenly crave a drink of water. He stood and headed downhill. There was always a stream or creek in a ravine. He arrived at a row of bushes, the plant life that lines such streams. In this case, though, they were all black or dried brown. When he pushed his way through them, his heart sank. The streambed was there, all right, but it was dry. This was August, long after the snow pack had melted off and the California drought had been even more severe this year than last.

He hiked back up to where the bags were. There was one source of water there. He reached into his bag and pulled out a large fanny pack. This was his geocaching bag. He'd hoped to grab a cache or two in the Las Vegas area after his testimony, so he'd thrown his pack into his suitcase. He always kept a bottle of water in that bag. He unzipped the bag and extracted the bottle. It was unopened. He had one full bottle of water, so he wasn't going to die today. He opened the bottle. He was tempted to take a long drink, but he checked himself and limited it to a short swig. He screwed the cap back on.

He needed to make a plan, a way to get to help, or to get help to him. His life depended on it. He spoke the words out loud, "Cliff Knowles, you've been in rough spots before. You can get out of this."

Chapter 2

One week earlier

"Is the coffee hot?" Cliff asked. The question was directed at no one in particular, or, more accurately, to anyone who knew the answer.

"Yes," Ashley's voice responded. Cliff headed to the pot with his oversized mug. The pot was located on a small counter by the lobby front door, which necessitated him leaving his office. Cliff Knowles Investigations wasn't large enough to have a break room. Maeva and Ashley were the only other permanent employees, although they sometimes hired others for part-time or seasonal work. "But I have to warn you, it's pretty viscous."

Cliff poured some of the fluid into his mug and took a slug. "Vicious, I think you mean. It's awful." He poured the sludge from his cup back into the pot. "Make another pot." After a pause, "Please." He went back to his office.

"'Viscous'. Not bad. You took your SAT already. You heard back from your schools yet?" It was Maeva who made the remark.

"I didn't make Stanford." Ashley knew Maeva, the junior partner, had attended Stanford Law School for a semester and felt that band aid should be ripped off first. "But I made Davis and UDub. I'm waitlisted at Berkeley." Ashley was Cliff's niece and interning as his secretary part-time during the school year and full-time during the summer.

"Good schools all."

"I guess." Ashley carried the pot out the door to dump it in the bathroom down the hall, shared with any member of the public who made it to the third floor, but since it required a key, that usually meant clients of the law firm that took up most of the floor. She returned and started the pot brewing.

When it was ready, Cliff's nose alerted him to the fact. He inhaled the hearty aroma with gusto and emerged from his office with mug in hand once again. As he was pouring, the office door opened. A young man entered carrying a small pouch, a sort of satchel. He was short and had a receding hairline although he couldn't have been older than twenty-five. He had a

Brillo pad beard and tattooed calves, which were visible since he was wearing shorts.

"Is Cliff Knowles here?" he asked Ashley, whom he obviously tagged as the receptionist since there was a nameplate on her desk reading 'Reception'. Cliff was obscured from the man's view by the door, which opened inward toward the counter. Cliff said nothing. He knew he had no appointments and didn't like dealing with strangers who showed up unannounced.

"Do you have an appointment?" Ashley asked, although she already knew the answer.

The man stepped forward, right next to her desk. "No. Can I wait?"

Ashley instinctively cast a glance at Cliff. A more experienced receptionist might have resisted the urge, but it didn't matter. The result was inevitable. The man turned around and saw Cliff standing between the door and the counter.

"Cliff Knowles, you've been served." The man handed some papers to Cliff. Cliff didn't take them, so the man touched them to Cliff's arm and dropped them on the counter. He walked out of the office.

"Oh, crap. I'm sorry, Cliff," Ashley said.

"Couldn't be helped. He'd've seen me when he turned to leave, even if you'd gotten rid of him. I'm too fat to miss." Cliff was sizeable, but most of the bulk was muscle, not fat. He worked out with weights regularly.

"I never said you were Cliff. You could have told him you were someone else."

Cliff shot her a look and tapped his mug with his free hand. "Cliff" was emblazoned in gold on the side contrasting with the royal blue background that completed his Cal colors. He took the papers and his coffee and went into his office.

One was a subpoena to appear in state court in Las Vegas in one week. The other was a cover letter and check for air fare, enough to cover first class from San Jose to Vegas and back. He inspected the subpoena and became more confused the more he examined it. It was issued on a criminal case: State of Nevada vs. Van Truong. It had been issued by a private attorney, not the district attorney. He didn't recognize the name of the defendant. Why would a defense attorney want a retired FBI agent to testify?

And why was it Las Vegas? Cliff had never worked in the Las Vegas office when he was in the Bureau. His criminal cases had all been in the Bay Area.

He had business meetings planned and he hated the hassle of air travel. He had to at least try to get out of it. He looked up the number for the District Attorney in Las Vegas. He called and said he was a witness in the Van Truong case and needed to talk to the Assistant D.A. handling that case. He was put through surprisingly fast.

"Hello, Mr. Knowles. I'm Melissa Ingram, on the Truong case. I'm glad you called. Is this about the subpoena?'

"Yeah, what's going on? I don't know anything about any Truong." The irritation in his voice was not concealed.

"Believe me, I'm sorry you have to do it, but the defense is demanding you and Crosby show up in person. They issued the subpoenas, not me."

"Jim Crosby? He got one, too?"

"We've been notified that a subpoena has been issued for him, too. I don't know if it's been served yet. You don't remember the case? I can send you a copy of your 302 if you like, to refresh your memory. All you have to do is authenticate the recording."

"Recording of what?"

"Raven Tran's statement. It was eight years ago. I understand you may not remember it."

The memory came back to him now, jogged by Tran's name. It was a fugitive case. That's how the FBI classified it, anyway. To the Las Vegas police it was a murder case. Tran was a young Vietnamese gang member, the girlfriend of one of the leaders. There were four main players. One of the gang members had been knifed to death and the other three were all suspects. Tran's car was seen leaving the scene with a woman driving. Drops of the victim's blood had been found in Tran's car later, on the passenger side, tying her to the crime. The police had obtained an arrest warrant for her, but she'd fled the area. When leads suggested she'd been living in San Jose, a federal case had been opened at the request of LVPD.

In Bureau parlance such cases are known as UFAP cases, pronounced You Fap. It stands for Unlawful Flight to Avoid Prosecution. They constitute a substantial part of the FBI's criminal caseload and most agents get assigned such cases during their Bureau tenure. In bigger offices, there's usually a separate Fugitive Squad. They're popular cases among agents, especially the lazier ones, because there's no proof of anything required. The agent has to investigate to find the person, of course, but once in custody, the subject just gets shipped off to whoever wanted them. Agents don't even have to do that. The original agency, LVPD in this case, has to come pick them up. The agent gets statistical credit for the arrest, a "stat", and the case is over. It's much easier than trying to develop evidence and prove a case.

The case had actually been assigned to Jim Crosby. Crosby had located Tran and asked Cliff to come along for the arrest since Cliff was the only squad member in the office when the lead on her whereabouts had come in. Cliff hadn't known any of the details of the case, only that it was a UFAP-Murder case out of Las Vegas. What had made this case different was that when they picked her up and put her in the car, she said she wanted to talk. Most UFAP fugitives shut up and the agents sometimes don't even bother to Mirandize them. It's actually smarter not to. The law only requires Miranda warnings if the arrestee is being questioned. If you let them talk on their own, which happens occasionally, any statements are admissible.

At Tran's request they drove to the FBI office and settled in an interview room. She asked that her statement be recorded, another rarity. She said if her statement was recorded she'd be safer. She was afraid "Dice" would kill her if she was a live witness, but once her statement was already in the hands of the police, he'd have no reason to kill her.

Dice was the nickname of the gang leader. She told a story of how Dice had asked her to come along as driver while he and another member, Duck, taught a third member a lesson in loyalty. The victim was Mickey Mendoza, Dice's brother-in-law. Further details escaped Cliff's memory, but basically, she'd claimed she hadn't known there was going to be a murder, just a beating. She'd watched in horror as Dice and Duck returned to the car with Dice holding a bloody knife, or so she said. Dice had gotten into the front passenger seat, getting blood in her car, and told her to get out fast. She explained his nickname came from a threat he once made to dice up a rival and the fact he liked to carry a knife. She'd never seen Duck before that night and didn't know his real name. Cliff didn't remember the name Truong, but he presumed that Truong was Dice, or possibly Duck.

"You still there?" the D.A. asked.

"Yes, sorry. I was just going over in my head what I remember about that case. Is Truong Dice? Why don't you put Tran on the stand? You don't need the tape. Is she giving a different story now and the defense wants to impeach her with the tape? That'll make him look even guiltier."

"Yes, Van Truong was called Dice. Tran's not giving any story. She's dead. After she was brought back here, the P.D. didn't want to put her in witness protection because Truong was in the wind. He had fled and they didn't know how long it would be before any trial could take place, if ever. They couldn't house or guard her indefinitely. Duck was never identified other than as a Vietnamese male. The police had believed her, but she still participated and was guilty of felony murder. They only had her word for it about Truong. So they charged her with the murder based on her statement – your FBI recording. She clammed up and didn't cooperate any further. She had no record, so she was granted bail. That was back in Covid lockdown days when death rates were high in prisons and judges were reluctant to hold criminal suspects unless there was strong evidence they posed a danger. She was the driver, not the alleged killer, so she was granted bail. She fled again. Her body was found six months later in your area. An overdose."

"Is he being charged with her murder?"

"No. We don't have evidence for that. The murder case we're trying is the one eight years ago, the one Tran told you about. Mickey Mendoza is the victim."

"So what other evidence do you have?"

"We have some circumstantial evidence and forensics, but the recording is key."

"That was Jim's case, not mine. I don't remember it all that well. He wrote the 302. I signed it, too, and can swear to it, but that's about all. Why didn't you bring Jim out for a preliminary hearing to authenticate it there or in grand jury?"

"We couldn't do it before a grand jury. Dice was arrested on a Friday and had to be charged within forty-eight hours or released, so we had to proceed by information instead of indictment."

Cliff was a lawyer and former Legal Advisor for the FBI. He knew criminal procedure well. Prosecutors like to present evidence before a grand jury to get a subject indicted. The prosecutor is in control and defense doesn't get to present evidence, although the defendant does have a right to testify there without a lawyer. That option is almost never taken since his or her testimony can later be used at trial and his lawyer can't be present to object or frame favorable questions. The evidence is one-sided and it only takes a two-thirds vote to indict, so it's rare to get a no bill, the term for a refusal to indict. Grand juries don't decide whether someone is guilty, only whether there is enough evidence to warrant a trial. But grand juries have busy schedules and typically sit only one or two days a week, not on weekends.

The alternative is to proceed by the officer filing a criminal complaint, essentially a sworn affidavit, or a document called an information, which the prosecutor prepares stating the alleged facts and charges. The defense is entitled to a preliminary hearing to question the evidence in the case of an information or complaint, but usually not in an indictment.

"The recording speaks for itself. Tran laid it all out. You can't get it in without us?"

"I only need one of you to authenticate it. I called Crosby about this a week or so ago and he agreed to come out. It's the defense who's subpoenaed you both. The lawyer's probably hoping to get you two to tell contradictory stories to get the recording thrown out."

"What's to contradict? About all the 302 said is that Tran made this voluntary recorded statement on such a such a date in the FBI office witnessed by the two undersigned agents. All the facts are in her words on the recording. We don't have any personal knowledge of the truth of what she said."

"You're right. I don't understand their strategy. The defense has actually been cooperative so far, conceding the authenticity of other evidence. But the tape is key, like I said. And the subpoena is good in California, even though it's from a Nevada court. You know that, right?"

"Yeah, I know. Okay. I guess I'm stuck. I'll be there."

"I'm looking forward to meeting you."

Cliff hung up the phone and pulled out the directory of the society of FBI retirees. Crosby's name wasn't there. Not every retired agent joins. He thought back to what he remembered about Jim Crosby. Jim had been a good agent for fugitive work, but wasn't around much because he was a Bureau pilot and was often gone flying on surveillances for other squads or giving check rides for other pilots. Crosby had not been able to afford much of a house when he'd been transferred to San Jose. His entire time there he had been lobbying to get to one of the division's smaller resident agencies, or R.A.s. He'd finally succeeded and gotten transferred to the Eureka R.A. Cliff had heard he'd recently retired and was now a private flight instructor. That gave him an idea.

Chapter 3

Now - Friday

Cliff didn't think a rescue effort was likely to be mounted any time soon, and even if one were, he didn't think the wreckage could be seen from above with the ravine's deep shadows covering them. He didn't know where they were exactly or how far it was to civilization. His first task was to find out.

He pulled his geocaching bag from his suitcase. Inside was his handheld GPS receiver, a Garmin. It didn't have any connection to the Internet or the phone system, but it could receive satellite signals from the sky and tell him his location. He turned it on and scrolled to the satellite page. The graphic showed two small green icons in the circular graph. That meant it could "see" two satellites. Normally there were seven or eight or even more within sightlines. The walls of the ravine were blocking them. The device couldn't compute a location without at least three, and practically speaking, it usually took five or more. He'd have to wait until he got to an open spot. He turned it off. He didn't want to run the battery down on the Garmin. He had one set of spare batteries in the bag, but that was all, and searching for satellites ate batteries like a pothead gobbled sweets.

It was a cloudless sky and midafternoon, but the sun was on its way down and it would be darker soon. He decided it was better to stay where he was for now. Maybe there was a geolocator beacon broadcasting from the plane or someone witnessed the plane going down. A rescue effort may be underway. He thought it was a slim chance, but worth a night's wait. He also wanted to make a better sweep of the plane and the surrounding area for any survival supplies if he did have to leave the area, and that would have to wait until the fire burned itself out. After that he needed to get to water and open sky.

He opened his suitcase and extracted jeans and a light flannel shirt, his one change of clothes and what he'd planned to wear if he'd gotten a chance to go geocaching. It was over 90 degrees now, but they were in the mountains and he knew it would get cold overnight. The warmest thing he had to wear was his suit coat, but it obviously wasn't designed for rugged terrain. He couldn't find any serious damage to his coat or slacks and it was a two thousand dollar suit, so he didn't want to wear it if it wasn't necessary. He changed into the jeans and shirt and put his suit into his bag. It would get all wrinkled, but that could be ironed out.

Most of the rest of the stuff in his bag was underwear, socks, papers from work and a novel he was reading. He didn't have a spare pair of shoes, so he was going to have to make do with his leather dress shoes.

He opened Jim's bag. Jim had changed clothes at the courthouse and had been in casual clothes when the plane crashed. His slacks and sport coat were in his suitcase. Cliff decided he could use the sport coat as an extra layer. Cliff was a lot bigger than Crosby and knew he couldn't fit into it. There was a shaving kit, another change of underwear, a clean dress shirt, and a pair of dress shoes. Jim must have been wearing his tennies or hiking shoes when flying, but Cliff had no memory of noticing his feet. There was a laptop and a book in the bag but no phone.

Cliff turned on the laptop. It came to life. It didn't ask him for a password. The poor security disturbed him somehow, despite the fact that was good for him at this moment. There was no wi-fi signal, of course. The battery level was also down to less than 15%. There was a cord, but no place to plug it in. He couldn't see how it could help him, so he turned it off.

He checked over the space blanket for holes or other damage. It seemed fine, so that was an important survival item. He set it aside. He looked around and settled on a spot against the nearest ravine wall as his base for the night. He moved his meager stash there.

Then he walked back to the crash area. He stayed far enough away to feel safe if something exploded, but he wanted to make sure the fire wasn't spreading. The plane was crumpled against the rocky ravine wall. The only foliage near it was one charred bush and the branches the plane had knocked off the tree on the way down. The branches were burning, but slowly and nearly consumed already. The tree they'd come from was over thirty feet away. A few other trees grew farther down, but most of them looked charred and dead. There must have been a forest fire here recently. He was mostly worried about sparks flying to other parts of the ravine. Some areas had plant life starting to come back from the fire, but they'd be dry from the drought. There were flames and black smoke visible in the cabin along with a chemical stench. He assumed that the upholstery and plastics inside were burning.

This routine went on for three hours. The fire waned as he sat watching. Darkness fell suddenly, like someone had cut the power. The temperature began falling just as fast. He was growing thirsty and hungry. He treated himself to another swig of water, but there was nothing he could do about the hunger. His watch showed it was approaching 7:30, but the fire was clearly dying and there was nothing for him to do. He returned to his base spot, spread out Jim's coat as a mattress, curled up under the space blanket, and tried to sleep.

He awoke the next morning around sunrise. The sun hadn't penetrated into the ravine yet, but the sky was brightening enough for him to navigate. His hunger was worse than yesterday and his thirst worse than that. He took another drink of water, a longer one than before. The bottle was now one-third empty. The humidity was very low in these drought-ravaged mountains, and he knew his thirst would only grow.

He rose with difficulty. The rocky ground had made for a very uncomfortable night and he was paying the price now. He discovered he'd been bruised in the crash but was only feeling those bruises now. After relieving himself he made his way back to the plane. The fire was completely out but there was still warmth to parts of the fuselage.

The first order of business was Crosby's body. It was an unrecognizable blackened form now, which made it slightly easier for Cliff to deal with. Jim had not been a close friend, but he was a fellow FBI retiree and Cliff respected him. He pulled the branch free so that the pilot's body was no longer pinned. Once the remains were out of the plane, he checked the pockets and found a cell phone, but it wasn't operable. He looked around for a place to bury him, but there was no possibility of digging in this rocky environment. He settled on laying the body next to the plane. Covering it with rocks would take a long time and he didn't see the point. The FAA or someone would probably be doing an investigation of the site and he didn't want to disturb the scene any more than necessary.

He crawled into the wreckage. The destruction was near total. He found a water bottle by the pilot's seat, but it had melted into a blob and the water inside had boiled away. He scraped the blackness off the instrument panel and found what he was looking for. The plane had a GPS built in. Unlike Cliff's, which was turned off and in his bag, the plane's had been on during the flight. The screen was still partially legible. It appeared to still have power, probably from a backup battery. The reading would be the location where it had been when it lost contact with the satellites – right before the crash, in other words.

The latitude and longitude readings he could make out read N37 W119. The remaining digits were illegible. The numbers meant little to him beyond the fact he was somewhere in the California Sierras, a fact he knew already.

He returned to his own suitcase and retrieved his Garmin GPS. It had a map of California in it. He took it to the plane and programmed in the coordinates from the plane's GPS. His Garmin brought up a map of the area on the screen, but it was a high satellite view. The partial coordinates delineated a huge rectangle that encompassed most of the central Sierras including nearly all of Yosemite, Mono Lake, and stretching down almost to Madera in the Central Valley. But he knew that Jim had taken the route through Tioga on the way out and was going to do so on the way back. They hadn't made it through there yet, which meant he was in the northeast corner of the rectangle, on the eastern side of the Sierras. That was a triangle roughly bounded by Mammoth Lakes, Mono Lake, and Highway 120 at Tioga Pass.

Highway 395 was probably the closest main route. He thought that was to the east, but couldn't be sure. He didn't have the luxury, or the burden, of making a decision. There was only one direction he could go – north. That was the downstream direction and the only exit from the ravine. He gathered his gear, including the gun and ammo, and surveyed it. He inserted one magazine into the gun and racked the receiver, loading a round into the chamber. There was no point in carrying an unloaded gun. He put the second magazine into his geocaching bag along with the gun, but he didn't include the extra ammunition. Bullets are heavy and he felt two magazines would be plenty.

The lighter stuff was wrapped in the space blanket to make a bindle. This included his book. It was too big to fit in the fanny pack and he considered leaving it behind due to its weight, but he had a vague notion that he might be able to use the pages as kindling for a fire. The suitcases were too awkward to carry. He was able to detach a strap from one of the suitcases and use it to tie the bindle securely. He could at least sling this over his shoulder, but most of its weight rested on the fanny pack around his middle.

He set off to find water, food, and shelter.

Chapter 4

One week earlier – Friday
The Palo Alto FBI Office

"I need to ask you a favor." The caller was her husband.

"Cliff, I don't like the sound of that." Ellen Kennedy was well aware from past experience that her husband played fast and loose with FBI rules in aid of his private investigations business. Unlike Cliff, though, Ellen was still an active FBI agent and could be fired for bending them.

"No, it's legit. I've been subpoenaed on one of my old cases."

"Yeah, so what's the problem?"

"I need you to look up the home and cell numbers for Jim Crosby. He retired out of the Eureka R.A. about three years ago."

"He's retired. Isn't he in the directory?" The directory she referred to was the one listing members of the association for retired FBI agents.

"No, I looked there. Not everyone joins. He's been subpoenaed in the same case. I thought he might want to travel together. We can refresh our memories on the case."

"I remember him. Just a minute." She pulled an old office directory from her desk and found Crosby's cell number. After giving it to him she asked, "What kind of case is it?"

"UFAP-Murder out of Las Vegas."

"You didn't work fugitives. What's the story?"

"It was Jim's case. I was just a spare body for the arrest and I sat in on an interview. The subject talked and even made a recording. All I'm doing is authenticating the tape."

"That doesn't take two people."

"The defense issued the subpoenas. I guess they want to try to get us to contradict each other, make the tape sound unreliable. That's one reason I want to travel with Crosby."

"When is it?"

"Next Friday. The hearing's in the morning. We should fly in Thursday and fly out right after the hearing. I'm sorry that'll leave you with the kids for one night."

"I can handle it. I've done the same to you often enough."

"Love you."

"You too. See you tonight."

Cliff called Jim Crosby and left a message. Crosby called back several minutes later.

"Hey Cliff. Jim Crosby returning your call. Sorry I didn't pick up. I didn't recognize the number."

"No problem. Hey, did you get a subpoena from the defense in the Truong case?"

"Yeah, I did. How did you know? You got one too?"

"Right."

"What the hell? What do they need you for? It was my case. I talked to the D.A. a couple of weeks ago and agreed to fly out and authenticate the tape."

"I guess they hope we'll get our stories crossed somehow and get the recording tossed."

"What stories? That was one of the shortest 302s I ever wrote. We arrested her, Mirandized her, and she asked to make a recording. She even signed the Miranda warning form and said on the tape she'd requested to make the recording. The D.A. said they have the form, so that's not an issue. I didn't write up anything she said. The recording speaks for itself."

"Who knows. The D.A. said she didn't understand the point. I suppose if they get the recording tossed somehow, then we'll have to testify as to what she said."

"Won't that be hearsay?" Crosby asked.

"Yes, but there's an exception to the hearsay rule. Two, in fact. It was a statement against penal interest. She admitted to participating in the crime. Second, she was a coconspirator with the defendant, so it's considered like his own statement. Hearsay is allowed."

"They paid you the travel fee?"

"Yep. That's what I was calling you about. I figured you'd be flying down there in your own plane."

"I was planning to. You want a lift?"

"I'd much rather fly direct with you than go through airport security and all that crap. We could talk over the case in the plane. You can have my fee."

"I'd be happy to have the company. Keep your money. If you pay to refuel in San Jose, that'll be good enough. That'll save me some. I need the hours anyway to keep my rating. You're actually doing me a favor, and you're almost on the way."

"It's a deal."

They made arrangements to meet at a local airport the day before the hearing.

Now -Saturday

Ellen woke up early and rolled over. Cliff's body wasn't in the bed. She could tell he hadn't been in it. She had gone to bed last night irritated that Cliff hadn't called or texted to let her know the hearing had gone late and he would be arriving late. She'd assumed that he would arrive around midnight or so and get in bed. That obviously hadn't happened. Now her irritation turned to concern.

She unplugged her phone and looked for a text or email. There were several, but none from Cliff. She could hear that Tommy was already up and watching cartoons in the living room. Mia was probably still asleep. She got up and took care of her morning ablutions then went out to tend to the kids.

Once Tommy and Mia were ensconced in play, she called Cliff. The phone went right to voice mail. This in itself wasn't too alarming. Cliff had warned her that he might have to stay over until Monday and if so, he might go geocaching on Saturday. But he always took his phone geocaching, so that didn't really explain why he had the phone off.

She called the office weekend duty agent and explained that she needed the personal numbers of Jim Crosby, his wife if he had one, and whoever was the current duty agent in Eureka. The duty agent questioned her about why, and eventually looked them all up for her. Jim Crosby was divorced, it turned out, and there was no number for his ex-wife.

She called Crosby's number first, but it, too, went straight to voicemail. He might not be picking up since he wouldn't recognize her number. Next she called the duty agent in the Eureka R.A.

"Sheila York."

"Sheila, this is Ellen Kennedy in the Palo Alto R.A."

"Oh, hi, Ellen. What's up?"

"Did you know about Jim Crosby going to Vegas on a case?"

"He had to go to Vegas? No. He didn't check in with me or Ben." Ben was the other agent in Eureka. There were only two to cover every coastal county north of Mendocino. "Why?"

"He and my husband were subpoenaed to Las Vegas on an old UFAP case. They were supposed to be back yesterday evening, but Cliff didn't show up and didn't call or text."

"Hmm. I see. Do you want Jim's number? I'm sure we have that."

"No, I have that already. I called. Both phones go straight to voice mail."

"Who's the contact in Vegas? There'd be a duty AUSA you could call."

"It's a local D.A., not an AUSA, but I don't have a name or number. It's a Saturday, so I doubt I could get in touch with them."

"Do you know the hotel where he was staying?"

"Yes. Thanks. That's a good idea. I'll call them."

"Hang on. Maybe Jim didn't pick up because he didn't recognize your number. I'll call him. I know I'm in his contacts. He'll answer." She put Ellen on hold for two minutes, then came back on. "No answer."

"Do you know if he has relatives who would be looking for him or expecting him to call or text when he got home?"

"No, sorry. He's divorced. If you need me to do anything, let me know. I could roll by Jim's house, but I don't know if that would prove anything if he's not answering his phone."

"Sure. Thanks. I'll call you if I need to."

Ellen said goodbye and called the hotel. The clerk there told her that Mr. Knowles had checked out Friday morning.

Two days earlier – Thursday

Cliff and Jim landed at Clyburn Executive Airport south of the city and Jim rented a car. Both men checked into a hotel near the courthouse. Crosby had relatives in Las Vegas, so he left in the rental car to visit them. He told Cliff he'd meet him downstairs for breakfast the next day.

After checking in, Cliff called Ellen to let her know he'd landed safely and gave her the room number at the hotel. It was still light out and he had a few hours to kill, so he decided to do a little geocaching within walking distance of the hotel. Downtown geocaching wasn't his favorite style, but there were some interesting caches nearby. He began to check them out on his phone app.

Lazy Daisy had over seventy favorite points and wasn't far. That's a lot of favorites points. It's been around since 2008, so that may explain it to some degree, but he figured it would be a good one to start. Neonopolis was another one with over thirty favorite points. It was hidden in 2015, so on a point per year basis it was almost as popular. He put those on his list. He wasn't interested in accumulating find numbers any more. That was something for newbies. He just used geocaches to introduce him to some interesting areas when traveling. He downloaded a few more geocaches and set out on foot.

After doing those two caches he couldn't help but check out the Fremont Street Experience. It was like landing on Mars and finding it peopled by alien creatures. By that he meant gamblers or tourists who were just blown away by the glitz of casinos. The city had covered two blocks of Fremont Street and turned it into a pedestrian mall. Casinos dominated the space, but neon lights permeated the whole mall blasting out enough lumens to shame the sun. Vendors hawked sunglasses, kettle corn, and souvenir T-shirts. A tattoo parlor and "licker" bar managed to sandwich themselves between the casinos. Corpulent couples and half-dressed teens gawked and giggled at it all, cell phone cameras at the ready as they meandered through. Good taste was apparently prohibited on the premises. The predominant style on the girls seemed to be slattern chic. The tattoo parlor displayed a sign saying "Tattoos while you wait." He wondered what the alternative was. He eventually realized he was one of those alien creatures and decided to get back to the hotel for dinner.

Crosby had called Melissa Ingram to let her know they'd arrived and would be at the hearing the next morning so he didn't have to take care of that. He ate in the hotel and spent the evening going over some paperwork from the office and watching television in his room.

Chapter 5

One day ago – Friday

The two retired agents arrived at the Lewis Street courthouse and were put through the usual security screening. They were directed to Melissa Ingram's office.

"Jim and Cliff? Thank you guys for showing up." They each raised a hand as she mentioned their name so she'd know who was who.

"It's part of the job. Even after it's not our job," Crosby observed.

"I let the defense attorney know you were here. I'll take you to the courtroom, but you'll have to wait outside on the bench until you're called in. It's a full calendar and we're still way behind with delays ever since Covid. We may not get started on time. Sorry if that happens."

"No problem," Cliff said.

"Normally I'd go over your testimony before going in, but I've got a witness in another case coming in I need to prep. You guys are pros and there's nothing to prep you for, really."

"Are you going to call both of us?" Cliff asked.

"No, just Jim. Once the recording is in, that's all I need."

Crosby knitted his eyebrows in a troubled look. "Is this about the Miranda warnings? Because she was given the warnings. She signed the form and said on the tape she was talking at her own request and had been given the warnings."

"No. You're right. We're solid on that. Dice doesn't even have standing to challenge them anyway. His rights wouldn't have been violated if you hadn't given her the warnings."

Cliff's lawyerly mind was unsatisfied. "I still don't get it. Why did they subpoena me? Do they think they're going to get one of us to say we held a gun to her head and forced her to make a false recording?"

"I have no idea. I don't get it either. The judge would never believe anything like that and wouldn't even let them go there without providing some evidence of it first. I guess we'll just have to wait until the hearing. I have to go. Why don't you just hang out in the break room across the hall until I come get you."

The two men did exactly that. Cliff saw bagels left out by some generous employee. He was tempted – he was always tempted by food – but a bagel meant coffee, too, and his FBI experience had taught him that you didn't want to fill up with coffee before getting on the stand. In fact the very thought spurred him to seek directions to the men's room.

Fifteen minutes later Ingram came to fetch them. They exited the elevator and shouldered their way through the crowded hallway. She pointed to the bench outside the courtroom and gave an apologetic shrug since it was already occupied. The men stood there people-watching and chatting about old FBI friends while Ingram disappeared into the maw of the courtroom.

Twenty minutes later she came out again.

"It's over. You guys can go home."

"What?!" Crosby growled. "I didn't even testify. Did the tape get in?"

"Okay, let's go to my office and I'll explain. It's getting weirder and weirder."

They retraced their steps to her office. She put her finger to her lips signaling silence while they were in the elevator so they wouldn't be overheard. Every courthouse has its spies.

Once in her office she began, "It's good news and bad news." The two agents looked at each other.

"Okay, I'll bite," Cliff said. "The good news…?"

"He's bound over for trial. The defense waived the preliminary hearing and stipulated that probable cause exists to hold him."

"So the tape is in? I'm done?" Crosby said.

"Sorry, no. That's the bad news. You'll have to come back for the trial and authenticate it then."

"Well what the hell? We're here now. Why didn't you tell the judge the witnesses were ready to testify?"

"I did, of course. I argued for it strongly. I didn't want to put you through this again. But Bollinger, the defense attorney, apologized and said he had another case in another courtroom he had to get to and that the cross-examination of you two would be quite long. He pointed out he was paying the travel and per diem costs for both of you, so it was no burden for you or the state to bring you out again. He agreed to subpoena you again and pay the fees then. Normally this judge would allow me to put you on regardless out of courtesy to you, but he's so backed up with cases since Covid, he accepted the defense waiver and bound Truong over for trial. It's become a real rocket docket lately. He said by trial there'd be more time for cross. He asked me to apologize on the court's behalf to you guys."

"Have you ever had this happen before?" Cliff asked."

"No, not on a murder case. I've had the defense waive prelim, of course, but it's normally only after bail has been granted and never on the day of the hearing. His client is in jail without bail. If he was going to challenge the tape, now's the time to do it. If he'd been successful, his client goes free."

"Did you check to see if the defense attorney really had another case to get to?"

"No, but I can't see why he'd lie about it. It would get him in Dutch with the judge if the judge found out, and this waiver hurts his client here. Not only that, but it costs money to fly you guys out twice. You got your statutory fees, didn't you?"

"Yes, first-class, in fact," Cliff said.

"What?" Jim said. "You got first-class fare? I only got business class bucks."

"This isn't making sense," Ingram said. "He didn't have to pay you Jim, at all. I had you on my witness list so he knew you were coming out at state expense. I couldn't proceed without you. And you say it was a check, not a ticket? That's not normal. All I can say is soak him on the hotel minibar fees. And I'm not going to cry for you. We sent you an economy class ticket, and we can't get that back even though the defense paid you, too. One economy class plus one business class is more than Cliff's first class ticket."

"Yeah, I cashed that ticket. Cliff and I flew in my plane. We split the cost. We actually came out pretty sweet. That's a consolation, I suppose. The asshole's getting screwed in the pocketbook. It's still a pain in the ass. At least I can visit my brother at his expense."

"Will I have to come out, too?" Cliff asked.

"I don't need you, assuming Jim can come out, but you may get subpoenaed again by the defense. His only hope at trial is to get that tape thrown out. I really think this is all a ploy to get some leverage on plea bargaining. He wants me to think he's got something to get the tape tossed and hope I'll come down on the sentence recommendation or reduce it to second degree. He's probably just stalling, hoping I'll get nervous and bend."

"Okay," Cliff said, "so he's overpaid us and is going to do it again, but then he just gave up his chance to cross-examine us now? He really wanted us out here for some reason, and it's not for that. Has a trial date been set?"

"No. The clerk's office will notify us of the date in a few days. They're running about three months out right now. I'll let you know."

Crosby shook his head. "There's no point in speculating. Let's get out of here. The weather's good and it's only going to get worse this evening. Have you checked out of the hotel?"

"Yeah, but my bag's there," Cliff replied. "I don't need to change, but I have to go by and pick it up."

"My bag's already in the trunk of the car. Let's get back to the hotel and go."

Ingram thanked them both. They left the courthouse and walked back to the hotel. Crosby drove them back to the airport and turned in the rental car. Once the flight check was over he got clearance from the tower and taxied out. The takeoff was normal and the weather was perfect. They were on their way home and it wasn't even noon yet.

Six hours earlier – 5:30 AM

Van Truong woke. The cell phone he'd bribed the guard to bring him had woken him from an untroubled sleep. He had the cell to himself, another perquisite from the corrupt guard. Even so, he spoke in Vietnamese just in case. Prisoners in adjoining cells might overhear.

"Yeah, it's me, Dice."

"It's done. I got it done. I told you I could." The man speaking was Duc Bui. He worked at Clyburn Executive Airport as a mechanic. At least that was his official position. His unofficial position was as Dice's number two and in charge of the receiving operations for stolen goods. The gang put together raids on malls in California. Five or more members, men and women wearing face masks, black shirts and pants and hoodies, would pile out of a van, run into a high-end store like Gucci, and grab everything they could, then run out and hop back in the getaway van. The process takes only a few seconds. The goods are then flown to Las Vegas where Bui is in charge of receiving the goods and getting them to a warehouse where Dice took over the disposition.

"They both came in Crosby's plane. I got into it like I said."

"You plant it?"

"The cork's in place. No fuel can come out of that tank. He's already fully fueled and will think he has enough to get back, but half of it's stuck."

"Track them. I want to make sure it goes down. If it doesn't, we'll have to send someone after them both and that isn't going to be easy. This is the only time they're going to be together. If one of them gets hit first, the other's going to be put under protection. How long you think it'll take?"

"No way to know. They shouldn't notice it during takeoff. But if they detect something wrong, they'll come right back. I'm pretty sure that won't happen. The real question is when the pilot notices the fuel level hasn't changed."

"I thought you said you could fix that."

"I did, but only at the full position. The gauge will always show full. It will just look stuck. That's a bit suspicious, but he filled up last night when he arrived, so he thinks he's got enough fuel to get to San Jose. He's got an old Cessna with limited range with the weight he's carrying. They're both big guys. He can't fly over Mount Whitney. He probably doesn't have enough oxygen. His flight plan shows him going north to Tioga Pass and then cutting west to San Jose. I tweaked his engine to run rich, too, so he'll consume fuel more rapidly. If he notices the gauge before that, he might have someone look at it then, but he shouldn't be able to tell his fuel level is down. If he doesn't, he should run out of fuel somewhere in the eastern Sierras before Tioga."

"So can you track them or not?"

"Yeah, yeah. There's a website for that. You can track almost any plane in the air, at least here in the U.S., unless the pilot blocks the flight data for privacy. He doesn't normally block it. We researched this. He always files a flight plan and doesn't block his data. But the website's not too accurate. It will only show approximately where he drops off the grid. I also put a phone in the tail section in the first aid kit. If he lands or crashes within range of a cell tower, I can find it with the location sharing app I installed, but I can't be sure if the battery will last or the phone will survive a crash."

"This better work. My lawyer says there's no way for him to keep the tape out of evidence. I'm looking at twenty years or even life."

"Like I said, we researched this. Crosby has been flying in and out of Clyburn for years. He's got family here. The trick was getting the other guy on the same plane. We lucked out."

"It wasn't luck. I told the lawyer to send him a fat check instead of a round-trip ticket. That way he could keep the cash and fly with Crosby. It worked. Now you just do your job."

"I got it, boss."

Chapter 6

Now – Saturday morning

Cliff was picking his way down the ravine when his foot dislodged a rock the size of a basketball. It ping ponged its way down the side of the stream bed and landed with a heavy clunk on the rocks below. He realized for the first time how dangerous the terrain was. There was no trail, no path. He was climbing over rocks with his dress shoes. The distance to the bottom of the stream bed wasn't great – maybe thirty feet or so – but it was enough to disable him if he fell.

The way ahead was opening up. The rock walls were farther apart here than back at the crash site. It was more of a canyon than a ravine here. He stopped and tried his GPS unit one more time. It saw three satellites this time, but it still wouldn't bring up a map. Once again he decided to save the battery life by turning it off.

He thought back to the flight. The beginning had been normal enough. At least he had thought so. But there had been that one incident.

"Shit. The fuel gauge isn't working. It still reads full."

"You filled it when we landed."

"I know. We should have plenty, but not a full tank. We've been flying for hours."

"What do you want to do about it?"

"I'd land if I could, but we're over the Sierras. I don't know where there'd be any place to land here. I'll get a vector."

Jim had radioed air traffic control and asked for routing to the nearest airport. When asked whether he needed an emergency landing, he'd said no, the plane was flying fine but his fuel gauge was malfunctioning and he wanted to make sure he knew how much fuel he had. The controller had told him Mammoth was the closest airport with full services. Crosby had replied that he'd land there to check it out.

Three minutes later the engine had died. They were out of fuel in the one tank that wasn't plugged. The other one had plenty, but Duck's cork had plugged the line from that one. They turned into a glider in an instant, a rather bad glider. Jim had warned him to buckle tight and brace for impact. He didn't remember anything after that until he came to in the plane. He was still amazed that Jim had found a tree to hit in that barren rock-strewn hellscape.

He retracted the thought immediately. It was a hellscape for him now at this moment, and certainly for Jim Crosby. But the country was beautiful. He took a few moments to appreciate it. It was a stark, rocky environment at this elevation, not the carpet of green farther down, but the magnificent peaks held a grandeur of their own.

The incident with the fuel gauge kept nagging at him. This had to have been sabotage. Someone had sabotaged the tank. The malfunctioning fuel gauge couldn't have been a coincidence. That's what convinced him it was sabotage.

It all made sense now. The murder case depended entirely on the recording, and the recording was unimpeachable. If Truong had gone to trial with that tape in evidence, he'd have gone to prison for life. But with Raven Tran out of the way, that left Crosby and Knowles as the only two witnesses who could authenticate it. Get them together in one plane and crash the plane. Problem solved. Cliff remembered hearing that Stalin's favorite quote was "You have man, you have problem; you have no man, you have no problem." The preliminary hearing had been a sham. There was no way they wanted it to go forward. Once authenticated, the tape would have been put in evidence and therefore usable at trial with or without them and the game would have been over. Truong had just wanted to lure the two agents to Las Vegas so he could get rid of them both. Cliff wondered whether Truong's lawyer had gone along with it or was just taking orders from his client with no knowledge of the assassination plan. He feared it was the former.

His attention turned to his predicament. One thing he hadn't brought was a hat. It hadn't mattered before because the narrowness of the ravine had kept the ground in shade. The sky had been no more than a sliver. But now with the canyon widening and the sun rising, he'd entered full sunlight. The temperature was climbing fast while he was descending slowly. He pulled a T-shirt from his bindle and fashioned a wrap over his head.

He picked a path that maximized the shade and kept moving.

Now - Saturday morning

Ellen became seriously worried. Cliff had left the hotel on time Friday. It's now twenty-four hours later and he's not home and hasn't called. There's no guarantee the plane left, though. Maybe there was a mechanical problem or other delay. He would have called.

She went to the computer and searched "how to find out if a private plane left". The links all came up to flight tracking sites. Apparently some transponder or other doohickey on the plane reported its position every so often through satellites. The website query required the tail number of the airplane, something she didn't know. She saw that it was also possible for a pilot or plane owner to block tracking. It was unlikely that the plane was now in the air a day after it was supposed to be. She decided it wasn't worth trying to dig up the tail number from somebody.

The FBI stationed one agent at the San Francisco International Airport and it was someone she knew well. He was a reliable guy who often came by the Palo Alto office for training or other purposes. It was easier than going into the San Francisco office and relatively free of the drama at the main office. She looked up his cell number and gave him a call.

"Hello."

"Hal, it's Ellen Kennedy."

"Oh, hi, Ellen. To what do I owe the pleasure?" No chit chat. Let's get right to business. That was Hal.

"Look, Cliff was supposed to fly back from Las Vegas yesterday with Jim Crosby. They were testifying on an old case. He never showed up and hasn't called. I'm worried. Is there a way to find out if they took off?"

"Sure. What airline was it?"

"Oh. No. Crosby was flying his own plane. He picked Cliff up in San Jose and was going to drop him off there."

"Oh, right. Crosby is a pilot. Do you have the tail number of his plane?"

"No."

"Do you know if he filed a flight plan?"

"No."

"Do you know which airport he would have left from in Vegas?"

"There's more than one? I don't know. I just thought there was only one."

"Private planes often land at smaller airports like Palo Alto. I don't know what airports are around Las Vegas."

"I don't know. Sorry. Can you help?"

"Okay, let me see what I can do. I'll call you back."

It helps to know the right people. Hal called back a half hour later.

"Okay, Ellen, I was able to confirm they took off. Crosby filed a flight plan. Through logs the FAA confirmed the plane left from Clyburn, a smaller private field south of Las Vegas, but I haven't contacted anyone at the airport or flight control. Do you want those numbers?"

"Yes, please. The tail number, too, if you have it."

He gave her the numbers. It took her two hours, but eventually she was able to confirm that the plane had left Clyburn with two souls on board, headed northwest for San Jose in accordance with its flight plan. Air Traffic Control had confirmed that Crosby's plane had followed its flight path to a point over the Sierras. The pilot had radioed in that he was landing at Mammoth Airport to check a faulty fuel gauge reading. The controller had told him he was handing off control to Mammoth tower. He thought he had received confirmation, but radio reception had been poor. He saw the plane begin descent on radar and had believed that it had landed.

Ellen's call had spurred action. The airport authorities and Civil Air Patrol quickly determined that the plane had not landed anywhere and in fact radar had shown it had descended too quickly for a normal landing. Mammoth tower had never taken control and wasn't tracking the plane. ATC had last logged it over the Toiyabe National Forest on the California side. The U.S. Park Police, U.S. Forest Service and three counties were notified of a possible plane down in their area. Unfortunately, no reports from ground observers had confirmed it. Even so, an aerial search of the general area was initiated.

Ellen knew there was nothing she could do to help find it. She had to leave it to the pros.

Chapter 7

Cliff came to a barrier of trees. The blackened trunks and limbs had apparently been washed downstream when the winter snows had melted and come to rest in a tangle between the granitic Scylla and Charybdis lining the streambed. There was no direct way over, under, or through it without climbing gear and a skill set Cliff didn't have.

He thought through his options. It was noon and he'd only made about two miles by his estimation. It was very rough going. He was down to half his meager water supply. He couldn't just sit there and give up. He remembered there had been a game trail about a quarter mile back. If he'd been geocaching, he might have considered it a geotrail.

The canyon was opening up, which meant the slopes up the sides weren't as steep as before. It would still be a rough climb, but to survive he would have to take the trail up the side and try to get past the blockage going along the ridge. He should be able to get a clear satellite signal up there, too.

When you're looking for water, going uphill away from a stream is seldom a good idea. But he had no choice. He reversed his direction and headed back toward the plane. Twenty minutes later he found the game trail and began to climb. He could feel himself getting weak from the exertion and the dehydration. He was still in full sun.

He made a decision to wait until the sun moved enough to put him back in the shade. He reluctantly hiked back down the trail to the dry streambed where he could find shade behind a rock formation. He sat in the shade and inspected his leg. The blood was dry. It had been only a trickle, but any loss of blood wasn't good when you're dehydrated.

He realized that if any searchers did find the plane and came through here, they wouldn't know he'd gone up this trail. He decided to use his time to build a cairn where the game trail went up the canyon wall. This should serve as a signal to any future searchers. There were plenty of rocks, but it was exhausting work lifting and placing them on the cairn. He kept the cairn to three feet. That should be large enough to draw notice.

After an hour the sun had moved far enough, so he started up again, but he had drunk from his water again. He hoped he'd see something like a stream from the top of the ridge. It took him three hours, but he eventually made it to a fairly open spot nearer the ridgeline. He was in open sun again, but at least he had a clear view of the sky on two sides. He turned on his GPS unit and waited.

The satellite screen came into view. One satellite. Two more. An excruciating two minutes of watching the spinning circle while it searched for more. Then a fourth. Another minute and a fifth. Coordinates appeared at the top of the screen. He pressed the save button. He now had one location he could retrieve. After another two minutes two more satellites came up. He switched to map view.

His heart sank. The screen showed nothing but a textured pattern he recognized as open undeveloped space, the pattern used for mountains, plains, and desert. He pushed the zoom out button. The same pattern filled the entire screen. He repeated this four or five times with no change. Finally he saw a line appear on the far right of the screen. Highway 395 was the closest road, as he had expected, but it must not be close. There were no trails shown on the map. He was in open country. He needed to go east, but the ridges ran north and south. He knew he couldn't keep going up and down the mountains. He had to get north, the downhill direction, until there was a way to turn east.

He checked the screen again. He was at 10,607 feet elevation. No wonder he was so tired. The air was thin here and the sun was vicious. He also had a nasty headache from the elevation. He'd been higher in the plane, but that didn't bother him there because he wasn't exerting himself. Vigorous activity at altitude, though, brought punishment. He wrapped the cloth around his head a little more tightly and turned off the GPS. It had told him precisely where he was, but not how to get to safety. He'd need his wits for that.

He had to make a choice. He could make his way laterally along this side of the ridge and get back down to the streambed past the blockage. The other choice was to keep going up to the top and reconnoiter the far side. Without a sign of water in "his" streambed, he decided the second option was more viable. Another hour of struggling brought him to a point where he could look down the other side.

He could see a ravine on the far side that had some green foliage in it, meaning water. It also bent slightly eastward. The bad news was that he couldn't see a safe way down. He'd have to travel along the ridge top until he found one.

Ellen grabbed her phone like a cat grabs a mouse. She wasn't about to let a call go by.

"Hello."

"Mrs. Knowles?"

"Yes." She used her maiden name, Kennedy, but now was no time to stand on ceremony. She recognized the voice as the man she'd spoken to earlier from the air search team.

"I don't have any solid news, but we may have something."

"Yes, whatever it is …"

"Sure, well, first of all, we still have no confirmed crash. The plane may have landed. That's good news."

"I hear a 'but' coming."

"Yes, it's not all good, but there has been a possible sighting."

"Tell me."

"A private pilot flying from Tahoe to Las Vegas saw another light plane flying northward. That plane was descending rapidly, which seemed odd as there was no place to land there and no real scenic or other reason planes would dip low there."

"Was it under control?"

"It seemed to be, according to the pilot."

"Where was this?"

"That's the bad part, I'm afraid. He doesn't remember exactly. It was a long way to the west of his position. It was between the Sierras and the Nevada state line. That's a rugged area. He estimated it was somewhere in Mono County, but he wasn't at all certain."

"That's the eastern side of the mountains."

"Right. As you probably know, there was a lot of fire activity there in the last two years. It's always very dry. The snow falls mostly on the west side of the Sierras."

"You're telling me that even if they landed safely, they'll die of thirst."

"No, ma'am. I didn't say that, but most of the streams on that side have run dry by now. There's just not much snow melt left and zero precipitation since March. Do you know if they had emergency supplies with them?"

"No, I don't. I, … we never talked about that. Cliff hates to fly commercial. The delays …"

"Well don't give up hope. It's only been about thirty hours since they took off. People have lived for weeks in the back country, and like I said, we don't have any confirmation of a crash. Maybe they landed on someone's barn and will walk out tonight."

"I wish I shared your optimism."

"We've notified the NRAT. It's a radar analysis team and part of the Civil Air Patrol. They're usually quick. We just didn't get word to them as soon as I'd like. Do you know if either of them is an experienced woodsman or outdoorsman?"

"My husband is a long-time geocacher. I don't know about Crosby."

"Geocaching. Hmm. Well, that's something."

Ellen could tell from the tone of his voice that the man didn't hold geocaching as the pinnacle of outdoorsmanship. Nor should he. Cliff was not a survivalist or even a camper, but he'd hiked in the mountains a lot over the years and survived some pretty harrowing situations. She may not have been optimistic, but she was nowhere near a state of hopelessness.

"Thank you for the call. Please contact me the minute you have more information."

"Yes, ma'am. I will. Stay calm."

Cliff continued to make his way along the ridge for another hour before stopping. It wasn't easy going, but he was getting used to the terrain. He often had to use both hands as well as both feet to climb over rocks or shove through dried out foliage. He finally found what looked like another game trail leading down to the other side of the ridge. He knew better than to try to go straight down. It was too steep. He walked at an angle, three steps forward to one step down. Then every few minutes he'd reverse direction in a switchback pattern, because hiking on steep ground with the same foot on the down side the whole way became too tiring to that leg.

By the end of the afternoon he was in shade once more and at the bottom of this narrow valley. Here was yet another dry streambed, but there was something different about it. The forest fire had come through here, too, but small shrubs and other greenery had sprouted up in and around the stream bed. Most of it was still green. He took off his geocaching bag and set his bindle on the ground.

He felt the ground where some green growth covered the stream bad. It didn't feel wet exactly, but it wasn't as dry and dusty as the other stream bed. There had to be moisture there. He searched until he found a flat rock he could use as a spade. He dug under the roots. The ground was soft there and it got darker as he dug lower.

After an hour of digging, he scooped out a trench of sorts about eight inches long and six inches deep. He could feel the moisture at the bottom now. His finger came up wet when he pressed it into the mud at the bottom. He'd finished the water in his bottle long before and knew it was critical to replenish it. He had to make this work, but he was exhausted and ravenous. He stopped to take a break. He lay down on a relatively flat stretch and was asleep within seconds. A prop plane did a turn over the canyon minutes later and left. Cliff slept through it.

Three hours later he awoke with a start. Hunger pains gnawed at him like a dog with a chew toy but the unbelievable thirst was worse. It was dark now and it took a few minutes for his eyes to adjust to the dim starlight. He sat up and went back to the trench. He put his finger in and pulled it out wet once again. This time, though, it was wet to the first knuckle. There was now a small puddle of water at the bottom. He was tempted to stick his face into the hole and lap it up, but a survival instinct told him that wasn't the best approach.

The puddle was too shallow to scoop up and he didn't have a container that would work, either. He had the empty water bottle, but that wouldn't work because it was too wide. He had to make the hole deeper and larger. He resumed digging with a renewed fervor. After another two hours the hole was ten inches deep and ten inches long. The puddle at the bottom was still only one inch deep, not enough yet. It was also muddy.

He had read about people lost in the back country. Survivors who had drunk ground water from mountain streams had suffered some serious problems. Giardia infection was common. So was heavy metal poisoning from the lead and other residues of mining that contaminated the Sierra watershed. The operative word, though, was survivors. These were people who hadn't died. Giardia and the rest could be treated later. Water, even heavily contaminated water, was better than death by dehydration.

The moon made its way over the rim of the mountain ridge. It seemed almost prophetic because at that same moment he got an idea. He opened his geocaching bag and dug around until he found what he hoped would still be there. It was.

Chapter 8

The evening was cool for a September night. Maeva was soaking in the hot tub when her husband, a Los Altos police detective, walked out to the patio to talk to her. He was holding a phone in his hand.

"Have you heard from Cliff?" he asked.

"Cliff? No. He left to testify in Vegas. He won't be back until Monday."

"This is Ellen so I answered your phone. She says he's missing."

"What?! Are you joking?"

Maeva took the phone as she climbed from the tub and put on a robe. Ellen didn't really want to talk long because she was waiting for the call back from the Civil Air Patrol or other authorities. She mainly just wanted to know if Maeva had heard from Cliff or knew anything.

"Maeva. I guess you've heard." Ellen sounded calm and stoic. At least she wasn't panicked.

"I just did. That's terrible. Have you heard from Cliff? What are the search people telling you?"

"Another pilot may have seen them. It's not confirmed, but somewhere around Mono Lake a small plane was descending fast."

"Landing or …?"

"They don't know. The guy who spotted it was very unsure of the location. We're talking hundreds of square miles and it may not be them. It may not have even been a plane he saw. It could have been a condor or something."

"Are you okay?"

"I'm as okay as I can be. Of course I'm worried."

"I can come over. Or I can get someone from the PD to …"

"No, no. That's not going to help. I have the kids. We're just having a normal Saturday so far as they know."

"They don't know yet?"

"I haven't told them. Daddy's gone on work. They're used to it."

"I wish I knew something. Is there anything I can do?"

"Not unless you have superpowers I don't know about."

"Someone should be with the search team. Would you like to go? We could watch the kids."

"No. I don't think there is a search team exactly. I mean, without a more definite location, no one's going to start a ground search. There's this group, part of the U.S. Air Force Auxiliary Civil Air Patrol, that does radar analysis. They're supposed to be very good. Once they get a location then maybe, but ..."

"Okay, well, you just let me know. You need anything, call."

"I know, Maeva. You're always there for Cliff. For us. I've got my sister, too, and of course the whole FBI family."

"Right. Okay, then. Hang in there."

"I will. Thanks again."

Maeva wasn't satisfied with the way the call ended. Doing nothing wasn't in her DNA. Cliff had gotten her out of tough spots, but more importantly, he'd become a close friend and wonderful partner. A mentor. He'd given her a job when she'd dropped out of Stanford Law School and he'd taught her the private investigation trade. Then he'd made her a partner. It was because of him that she'd met her husband. She owed him more than lip service and good wishes. If there was anything she could do, she was going to do it.

She wanted to see for herself what the news reports were. She logged onto a news site and searched Cliff's name. He was well enough known that his disappearance would probably raise some flags. Nothing came up in recent news. So she began entering terms about airplanes, missing persons, and Las Vegas. She found a news item on the local television news channel website.

The item was short and contained little more than what Ellen had just told her. A pilot and one passenger had left in a private plane from Clyburn Airport near Las Vegas Friday morning and had not landed at their intended destination. Air Traffic Control had lost track of them somewhere over the eastern Sierra Nevada mountains. An aerial search in the area had been initiated.

Maeva noted three things. They had left Friday morning. She recalled Cliff saying he would probably fly back Friday afternoon. So the hearing had been quicker than he'd expected. Second, he had flown in a private plane instead of a commercial flight. She'd been there in the office when the subpoena had been served. He hadn't said anything to her about a private plane. She knew he had the money for first class commercial. Cliff had remarked at the size of the check. These may not be significant, but her investigator's mind lodged them as noteworthy. At least she had a place to start if she was going to do anything. Clyburn Airport. Third, neither Cliff nor the pilot were named. Apparently the authorities had not released that information. They must have it because they were in contact with Ellen.

She looked up the next flight to Las Vegas and booked a one-way ticket. Then she told her husband she'd be gone early the next morning to help look for Cliff. He knew better than to protest.

Cliff pulled out of his geocaching bag a small plastic open-ended cylinder, a tube, really, about half the size of the cardboard tube in a toilet paper roll. In fact, it was two tubes, one of smaller diameter that fit inside the other to form a closed container. Inside was a small sheet of paper labeled "Log Sheet."

This was a spare geocache. A couple of years earlier Cliff had come up with an idea for a cool geocache. He'd enlisted one of his geocaching friends who was an engineer. Silicon Valley was overrun with them. Techies oozed from the pores of the Googleplexes and Apple spaceships like sweat from a fat teen on his first date. His friend had a 3-D printer. Together they'd designed and printed a geocache consisting of two nested cylinders, but with a twist. Literally with a twist – with many twists, in fact. The interior surface of the outside cylinder had a tiny protruding knob. The interior one had a maze of grooves on its outside surface. In order to close it, or open it, it was necessary to thread the knob into the grooves and twist left, right, up and down in the correct path, avoiding the dead ends, just like doing a maze, only blindfolded.

Once the design had been tested and proven to work, he'd had two more printed. The first one had been a popular cache when he'd hidden it. He'd received dozens of favorite points in the first few months it had been out. But it had proved to be fragile. Finders had been too impatient with it once they'd found it and had become frustrated. Finally someone had resorted to brute force to open it, and the tiny guide knob had been broken off. Cliff had replaced that one with his first spare, but that, too, had fallen to rough handling. He'd archived that cache after that, but he still had the third cache container. He'd kept it in his bag as a spare in case he'd come across a spot he felt just had to have a geocache.

He had another use in mind for it now. But first he had to get it open. When he'd first made the containers he'd recorded the pattern of grooves and memorized the sequence of twists and pulls and pushes needed. But that was two years ago. He hadn't tried to open it in years, and it was always a little sticky. He thought back and tried to bring up the sequence. Right, up right again. Up a long way past the first open groove, left. Long twist. Down. Right. Wait. That's not right. He wasn't sure. He pulled to open it, but it wouldn't come. He'd messed up the sequence.

He tried again, but once again the container wouldn't open. He had a certain pride in the design and didn't want to destroy his creation. It had been cool, alright. But pride goeth before the fall and he was falling big time. He pulled with all his strength, which was considerable. He heard the crack and the outer cylinder came free. The guide knob had broken off – Alexander's Gordian Knot solution. He opened it up and removed the log sheet. He had the first tool he needed.

Then he went back into his bindle and pulled out the second tool: a clean pair of tighty-whities. It was the cleanest piece of cloth in the bindle. He opened the empty water bottle and pushed the cloth through the opening about an inch. Then he took the geocache tube and placed it in the hole flat against the ground so the opening was under the surface of the puddle. Water flowed into the tube. He couldn't fill the tube completely – the water wasn't deep enough – but he was able to pull up two or three tablespoons of muddy water in the tube. He poured the water slowly through the underwear sieve. The mud in the water caused it to clog up almost immediately, but with patience he could see the water drip through and accumulate in the bottle.

The moon was still overhead and the old saw came to mind, "make hay while the sun shines," only, of course, water was the hay and the moon was the sun. He checked the mud hole and the water level was lower now. The hole did not fill up quickly. It took another twenty minutes for the mud puddle to be deep enough again, but then he repeated the process, moving the underwear to have a clean spot for the filter. He repeated this process for five hours.

He was shivering from the cold despite having wrapped himself in the space blanket. Nighttime at this altitude meant near-freezing temperatures even in August. He had to stop the activity and get more rest. He couldn't travel at night in the dark, which meant that's when he had to sleep. He'd accumulated about one cup of water in the bottle, not nearly enough, but it would keep him alive for another day – if he could keep it down. He took a swig. It tasted exactly like it looked: like muddy water. But his stomach didn't object. Quite the opposite. He immediately felt refreshed. He screwed the cap on the bottle and made himself comfortable on the ground again. He fell asleep in less than five minutes.

Sunday morning

Duc Bui had tried to call Dice, but it hadn't gone through. He knew Dice couldn't keep the phone on in his cell. He'd have to wait for Dice to call him. Finally, the call came.

"Duck, it's me. So what's the story?"

"The plane still hasn't been found. That's good news, I think. They brought in the Civil Air Patrol. They're going through the data. We should know soon."

"Okay. Nothing pointing to you, though, right?"

"Nothing. There is something else, though. This bitchy redhead just came in and is asking around. She says she's the partner of the big guy. She's questioning who was working here when they took off. She's writing down names."

"A private dick? I wouldn't worry."

"I'm not. But I'll have to cooperate or it'll be suspicious. Most everyone here has already been questioned by the sheriff. There's going to be buzz until it's found. It was a normal take off. No one saw anything unusual. But, you know, people are worried it could come back to here – bad fuel – something like that. No one wants trouble with the FAA or with private pilots. We depend on them. Jobs are on the line. If we get a bad rep …"

"Yeah, like Yogi Berra said, if they don't want to come, you can't stop them. So cooperate."

"Hang on. Something's going on. There's some noise up front. The boss is coming out. Can you call me back in ten?"

"Yeah. Go see if they found it."

Bui joined the gaggle of airport employees outside the manager's office. He was telling them the findings from the Civil Air Patrol's radar team. It hadn't located the plane on the ground, but they'd been able to pinpoint the exact moment the plane had begun its descent. That had resulted in narrowing the area where the plane could be, assuming it continued downward. They were already directing local planes to the area. Unfortunately, it was in the eastern Sierras where there were a number of deep canyons. The plane would be very hard to spot from the air if it went down in one of those.

Bui made note of the coordinates given by the CAP. He was itching to get to the location and make sure the agents were dead and to remove any evidence, like the cork in the gas line and the cell phone. But it would be suspicious if he left now, and in any event the location was still only a general area in rough terrain. He'd have to wait until the wreckage had been pinpointed. His regular days off were Monday and Tuesday. He could leave then if necessary.

Dice called him back and got the updated information. They agreed that the best plan was to sit tight for now. Things were looking favorable. As Bui hung up with Truong, he noticed the redhead talking to the airport manager. He walked over closer and pretended to be checking out something. He could overhear part of their conversation.

"Look, Maeva, I have to protect the privacy of my employees," the manager was saying.

"You've already given the list to the sheriff. It's not private. I'm a licensed private investigator. One of the men was my partner. He's missing. Be reasonable. Or compassionate at least. I need to talk to everybody."

"They've all been interviewed. Everyone cooperated. Nobody knew anything. Besides, you have no authority."

"No, but I think you're forgetting something. Cliff Knowles is famous. You remember the San Quentin Massacre case a few years ago? He's the one who solved it. The CBS van outside tells me there's going to be more press here soon and I'm going to be talking to all of them. I'd like to be able to say you're not hiding anything."

"You're threatening me?"

"I'm not threatening. I'm investigating."

"Okay, I won't give you addresses or phone numbers, but you can have a list of names so that you can know you've talked to everyone. I'll mark the ones who were on duty when the plane landed or took off."

"That's a good start. Thank you. It's very much appreciated."

They disappeared into the manager's office.

Chapter 9

Melissa Ingram was watching her daughter's soccer game when the call came. The number was the duty D.A. number so she had to take it. Her daughter was picking clover on defense anyway. She wasn't likely to miss a goal.

"Ingram."

"Can you take a call from a woman who says she's the partner of one of your key witnesses? She says it's urgent."

"Key witness? Did she give you a name? Of the witness, I mean."

"Knowles. Clifford Knowles."

"Knowles. Really. Yeah, I can take it." Maeva was put through.

"Hello?"

"Hi, is this the D.A. on the Truong case?"

"Yes, I'm Melissa Ingram. Who are you, please?"

"My name is Maeva Hanssen. I'm Cliff Knowles's partner. I need to know about what happened Friday."

"First of all, I don't know you. And second, why do you want to know?"

"You know he's missing, right? Both of them. Has the press talked to you yet?"

"What? No. What are you talking about?"

"The plane. Cliff and the other agent, Crosby. Their plane went down. They're missing."

"You can't be serious. I haven't heard anything. There was an airline crash? I'd have heard."

"It wasn't an airline. Crosby was a private pilot. His Cessna went down over the Sierras, but they don't know if it crashed. It might have landed or been disabled. Or they could both be dead."

The force of the statement buffeted her like a sucker punch. For a moment she was speechless. If both of them were dead, she had no way to authenticate the recording. The murder case would be dead. As she considered this, she realized that her concern should be for the men, not the case.

"I'm so sorry. If that's true, that's terrible. I'm sorry, but this is coming out of the blue. I can't verify who you are."

"It's on the news. You've got a phone. Just search his name. Search mine, too. You'll find some old links on cases I worked with him."

"Okay, yeah, sure, I will. But …"

It was working its way into her brain: the thought that she might be responsible for their death. The defense had devised a ploy to avoid getting the recording authenticated. Could she have been played? Would Truong have actually killed the two agents? Of course he was capable of it. He'd killed Mendoza and probably Raven, or had her killed. But FBI agents? And was it possible to cause a private plane to go down hundreds of miles away? The thought that her foolishness or naiveté might have led to this ate at her insides.

Maeva broke the silence. "Can I meet with you? I'm at the airport now, but …"

"I have to go. Meet me at my house in an hour. I'll text you the address." She hung up.

After the call Melissa stood nervously watching her daughter trip and fall as the opposing team's forward ran right by her and scored a goal. The game was mercifully over twenty minutes later. After the orange slices, she told her daughter they'd have to skip the pizza party. A pout and a protest caught the notice of another soccer mom who volunteered to take the girl to the party and drop her off at home after. Melissa thanked her and accepted.

Maeva's rental car pulled up to the curb in front of a tasteful suburban house that would be financially unattainable by an assistant D.A. in the Bay Area with its seven-figure starter homes. Of course here the garden was succulents rather than a lawn, but with global warming California lawns were quickly going the way of the pterodactyl and ten-minute showers. In Nevada, the home was probably on the modest side. She walked to the front door and rang.

Melissa invited her in and they sat in the living room. She'd already made a pot of coffee and Maeva accepted a cup. Without being prompted, Maeva pulled out her private investigator license and business card for Cliff Knowles Investigations. Melissa accepted the card and waved away the license.

"I'm sorry I didn't know about your partner until now," Melissa began. "I don't stay on top of the news on weekends. I've got a family and …"

"Don't worry about it. The news reports still don't say anything about them being in Nevada for testimony. They haven't been publicly named. You might not have pegged it as relevant anyway."

"Does he, uh, Cliff, have family? I don't even know these men. I'm sorry …"

"Cliff has a wife and kids. She's waiting by the phone for a call from the air patrol people. I don't know the other guy. He's someone Cliff worked with in the FBI. Can you tell me about the case?"

"You think it's connected to the case?"

Maeva gave her a searching look and said nothing. Melissa's hangdog expression told her the thought had already occurred to her. She was looking for Maeva to tell her it wasn't her fault for letting the men get set up. Maeva wasn't ready to do that. Not yet anyway.

"If I had thought … God, I should have made sure to get their testimony in evidence. I'm kicking myself."

"Just tell me about the case."

"The defendant, Truong, he goes by Dice, tops a gang. It operates through southern California and southern Nevada. They distribute drugs and fence stolen goods. They're behind some of those mass mall robberies, although they fence goods from one of the Compton gangs, too."

"So Truong is a Vietnamese name. Is it a Vietnamese gang?"

"No, not entirely. There are Chicano and white members that we know about. We don't have them all identified. The murder victim, Mendoza, wasn't Vietnamese but he was involved somehow."

"How is Cliff involved?"

"Eight years ago Truong and his girlfriend, Raven Tran, along with a guy named Duck, went to settle an internal gang dispute with Truong's brother-in-law, Mendoza. Truong ended up killing the guy. Tran and Truong fled the area; we don't know who Duck is, so we aren't sure if he fled. The FBI caught up to Tran in San Jose. Crosby and Knowles were the arresting agents. She was afraid Dice would silence her the same way, so she volunteered to give a statement. At her request they recorded her statement and we have that recording. She claimed she hadn't known there was going to be a murder. She thought Dice was just going to threaten Mendoza. She was the driver and didn't go in. She thought that recording would keep her safe since once the government had her statement, Dice would have no reason to kill her. Within six months she was dead, but we couldn't tie him or anyone to the killing. It was an OD and she was a meth user, so it could have been an accident, but she died of fentanyl poisoning, so we think it might have been intentionally spiked."

"What about Duck?"

"We haven't been able to ID him. She didn't know his real name. That was the first time she'd ever seen him. She said he wasn't a street thug or robber. He had some kind of legitimate job and didn't come to the parties or do drugs."

"So what do you need them for if you have the recording?"

"It hasn't been authenticated. Someone needs to say they took this statement from her, and that it was given voluntarily. It's not admissible in evidence until that happens."

"Why both of them?"

"That's just it. We don't need both of them. I only needed Crosby. The defense wanted Knowles there, too. That's who subpoenaed him."

"So a minute ago you said something about not getting the testimony in evidence. Didn't you already have the hearing?"

"Yes, but the defense pulled a fast one. They stipulated that probable cause existed to go to trial and waived the hearing. Neither of the men testified. I've never had that happen. The defense usually likes to have the officers testify at the hearing and then at trial when they testify again, they can find discrepancies with what they said at the hearing. The recording still hasn't been authenticated."

"So if both men are dead, you can't get it into evidence at trial."

"Right."

"So there's motive. You know the defense attorney?"

"I've worked with him, or, I mean opposite him, before. I never thought he'd be capable of knowingly setting someone up for murder. He's a legitimate defense attorney, not just some gang mouthpiece."

As soon as she said this, a resolve formed in her. She held up a finger as a signal to Maeva to hang on a minute. She picked up her phone and checked her text messages. Truong's attorney had texted with her about plea bargains earlier. She found his text and his phone number. She called him. Maeva sat silently.

After four rings, "Clyde Bollinger."

"Melissa Ingram here. We need to talk."

"It's the weekend. Can't this wait?"

"No, it can't. Did you set them up for a hit?"

"What the hell are you talking about?"

"Crosby and Knowles. Did you bring them out to be assassinated so you could get the recording excluded?"

"Assassinated? Are you crazy? You know I'd never … wait. Has something happened?"

"Their plane is missing. They were returning to California in a light plane and it never arrived."

"You can't possibly think I had anything to do with that. Or my client. Airplane accidents happen."

Maeva reached into her purse and pulled out a piece of paper. She handed it to Melissa. It was a letter on bond paper with Bollinger's letterhead. Ingram's mouth hung open in shock while she read it. This was the cover letter that had accompanied the subpoena and check Cliff had received a week earlier. Maeva had gone by the office the previous evening to pick it up. Cliff had left it on his desk.

When Ingram caught her breath, she tore into Bollinger once more. "Oh, I can think it. I'm reading a letter you sent to Knowles along with your subpoena. Quote: 'Enclosed is a check sufficient to cover first-class air fare round-trip from San Jose to Las Vegas but if you choose to travel via private plane or other method, you are entitled to keep the unused amount.' What the hell?! You encouraged him to travel by private plane and included more than the statutory amount? When have you ever done that before?"

There was a silence on the other end.

"Bollinger? You there? Answer me."

"Look, that wasn't my idea."

"Your client told you to include that phrasing?"

"I … I … what my client told me is privileged. I can't reveal what he said."

"Bullshit. You know the law. If it's part of a conspiracy to commit a crime, it's not privileged. And waiving the hearing so the agents couldn't testify? Did you really have another hearing in a different courtroom?"

"Look, I wasn't ready to do the cross. I've been too busy to prepare. So I stalled. It happens all the time. My lord, Melissa, believe me. I would never knowingly set up someone for murder. These are FBI agents, for God's sake. If you think I'm morally capable of that, at least give me credit for not being that stupid. Sometimes clients … well, you know the kind of clients I have. They don't let us in on their plans."

"I'll believe you were played by Truong if you agree not to object to admission of the recording if these witnesses can't appear."

"Look, I still have an obligation to my client. I could lose my license. Maybe the witnesses are okay. Let's hope they are. I think you're jumping to conclusions here."

"The hell with your law license. If they turn out to be dead, you're facing a murder charge." She punched the END CALL button and slammed the phone down on the table. Clearly she still had the instincts of the analog phone days.

Maeva gave her a few moments to compose herself. Then she brought up a photo on her phone and handed the phone to Ingram. "Are any of these people connected to your case or to the gang?"

The photo was the list of employees the airport manager had provided. Ingram skimmed through the list. "Not that I know of."

"A couple of the names are Vietnamese."

"I can see that. That doesn't make them gang members."

"I'm not saying it does. I'm just wondering whether Truong's inner circle is mostly Vietnamese. Tran is a Vietnamese name."

"Okay, I'm not saying it's racist to look closely at those names, but what evidence is there that anyone at the airport has anything to do with the disappearance?"

"If the plane was sabotaged, where else could it have happened?"

"I suppose that's true, but really, what happens more often – a small plane crashing from mechanical problems or from sabotage?"

"I don't know. How often does a defense attorney pay a subpoenaed hostile witness extra money and suggest they travel by private plane?"

This question shut Ingram up for a moment. It was unheard of. Bollinger had to have been trying to get Knowles to ride with Crosby in his Cessna. There was no other credible explanation, at least not in retrospect. And what other reason than sabotage could there have been for that? The only question was whether the lawyer knew what Truong intended or was just following orders without questioning the motive. She could think of a couple of pretext reasons Truong might have given Bollinger.

"Okay, so what's next?" Ingram asked.

"Apparently they've narrowed the search area down. They were getting specifics from the Civil Air Patrol as I was leaving the airport. When the plane is spotted, they'll let me know. I'm hoping that will be later today."

"Where is it – the area they're searching?"

"Just northwest of Mammoth Lakes."

"Mammoth? The ski area?"

"I think there's a ski area there, but they were looking at a map and I think it was north of there."

"I'd offer, but I've got kids and I could be of more use here, I think."

Maeva took an appraising look at Melissa Ingram. The lawyer was perhaps thirty-eight going on forty-eight and at least fifty pounds overweight. Maeva didn't think she'd be an asset in the back country of the Sierras and in any event, she was right. Maybe she could put some pressure on Bollinger or gang members through police contacts.

"Of course. I doubt I'd be of much use there, either, but I have to try to do something. That's why I'm here. Maybe you can reach out to the officers on the murder case. Do they have any informants or other intel on Truong?"

"I'll contact the detective right away and ask him to call you. His name's Slonsky. I'll let you know if they come up with anything. Do you want to wait?"

"No. I have to get back to the airport. It was Clyburn, by the way. That's a general aviation airport south of Vegas. I'll send you a copy of the list of names."

Chapter 10

Sunday morning

Cliff hauled himself to his feet. It was already late morning. He'd missed valuable hiking time in slumber, but he'd had to finish getting water. He took a quick look in the hole. It had filled higher overnight than it had been yesterday. Quickly he took the geocache container and scooped a full jigger of the muddy water and added it to the bottle through his makeshift filter.

Then his need to relieve himself drove him to find a spot behind a bush downstream. As he stood there, he realized how foolish it was to seek privacy behind the bush and as for "downstream," that only made sense in order to avoid contaminating your drinking water. When there's no visible stream that hardly matters.

His urine was dark yellow and not very voluminous. His thirst was intense and even more troubling. He knew his kidneys were having a hard time. After zipping up, he took a drink from the water bottle. Like the night before, the muddy taste didn't bother him, and his body told him it had been the elixir of the gods. His hunger pains had been terrible the previous night, but now he hardly noticed them. There was a dull ache, but nothing more.

He packaged up his belongings, hooked on his fanny pack, and began his trek down the streambed. His GPS reading the previous day had told him that there was no point in searching for his position or for a cell signal until he'd made at least five miles. In this terrain, that could take all day. He was just too deep in the canyon and wasn't going to use his energy to climb to the ridge line again.

The sun had warmed the valley air, but hadn't yet hit the canyon floor. He could make decent time in the shade, but he knew when the sun was on the streambed, he'd slow down.

Two hours later he sat for a moment. That's when he spotted it – a small, gray lizard. It was posed still on the gravelly surface, head erect. Cliff stood slowly. The lizard didn't move. With a speed that surprised him, Cliff stomped on the lizard hard. The lizard had tried to escape, but Cliff's $400 wingtip had nailed it cleanly.

Carefully he pulled the body out from under his shoe and held it in his hand. The lizard wiggled, so it wasn't dead. Cliff knelt down and held it against a rock. He picked up another rock and smashed the lizard until there was no doubt it had seen its last days. Standing again, he examined it. He steeled himself to eat it, but balked on his first attempt. He decided it was the head that got him.

He squinted so he wouldn't have to see it clearly, and bit the head off, then spit it out. He shoved the body into his mouth and swallowed. The creature didn't want to go down. Cliff began to gag. It took the rest of the water to help it on its way, but the lizard ended up going down and staying down for the count. Cliff's stomach greeted it with a truly other-worldly collection of sounds. His hunger pangs actually increased sharply, but he knew that if the thing stayed down, he'd be in a much improved situation. A little food can go a long way when you're starving. The lack of water concerned him more now that he'd emptied the bottle.

He wasted no time in setting off downstream. The sustenance and water enabled him to pick up his pace. By four o'clock he was exhausted, but confident he'd made at least four miles. There was still plenty of daylight, but a decision presented itself to him here. The thick greenery at this point hinted at water near the surface of the ground, which was invitingly soft in places. He hadn't seen many such clusters. If he went on he might not find another. He remembered how long it had taken him to collect the water last night. He decided that doing the digging now so he could sleep tonight was more important than another mile or two.

Having learned from yesterday's experience, he set up his digging operation without difficulty and within an hour had the hole in suitable shape. The soil was very wet at the bottom. He arranged the space blanket as a sort of cushion on some rocks and lay back to wait for the hole to fill.

He checked it twenty minutes later. To his dismay, there was little more than a trace of water, definitely less than the hole had produced last night. He dug the hole deeper. Then he probed the greenery until he found what seemed like a lusher spot. He spent another hour digging a second hole there. Once again he lay back, his muscles aching and his throat parched.

The second hole was more productive. Painstakingly he scooped and filtered for the next five hours, moving back and forth between the two holes. His water bottle was three-quarters full of the precious fluid and he simply could do no more. He took one small drink, lay back on the space blanket, and was asleep within two minutes.

It was dinnertime when the call came. Ellen's sister had come over with her kids and a pizza so that Ellen wouldn't have to go out for anything or cook. The cousins were greedily wolfing down slice after slice and didn't need supervision. Ellen moved into the bedroom. Her sister followed.

The searchers had located the plane. From the air they had been able to see that it had burned completely. It was in a deep ravine and not easily accessible. The caller had avoided getting to the bottom line as long as possible, but Ellen forced it out of him.

"Are there any signs of survivors?" Her tone was clear she would brook no further temporizing.

"I'm afraid not. But there's no sign of any bodies, either. It's possible they made it out.

"Have you sent in a rescue crew? A helicopter?"

"No, ma'am. The county SAR, that's search and rescue, team will mount an operation tomorrow morning."

"'Mount an operation'? You mean a helicopter. Why not send one now?"

"It's too risky. Under the evaluation status of the CAP it's been determined that trying to send someone down a rope from a helicopter is not warranted. It will be a ground team."

"Isn't warranted? Two lives are at risk. Isn't that what those teams do?"

"Yes, but not in this case."

"Why not?"

"The CAP has rated this crash … uh, unsurvivable That's just the technical term. It's still possible they made it out, but when they evaluate it that way, they won't risk a helicopter night operation. If the men did survive, they aren't going to still be there. They would have hiked out by now."

"Jesus. You think they're dead. Is it a rescue operation or a recovery operation?"

The silence on the other end of the phone gave her the answer.

When Maeva got back to the airport, it was after 4:00 and most of the earlier employees were gone. The ones on duty weren't the ones she'd seen before. The airport ran 24 hours a day, but evening and night operations were greatly reduced. She found the management and identified herself. She was able to obtain the coordinates of the plane's location from the staff. It was still a major topic of interest and activity with this shift. She also learned that a ground operation to recover the bodies would begin the next day. Upon close questioning, she found that there had been no confirmation anyone had been killed in the crash.

When she examined the spot on a map, her heart sank. It was too far away to get to that night. She'd arrive in the middle of the night with no place to stay and not be fit to join a rescue team after two or three hours of sleep in her rental car. She didn't have clothing for hiking in the mountains, either. She gave up on the idea of joining the SAR team. Instead, she called the Mono County Sheriff's Office and asked to be put in touch with someone on the search and rescue team.

"Hello. Forster."

"Deputy Forster, I understand you're part of the rescue team to recover the downed Cessna tomorrow. I'm the business partner and friend of Cliff Knowles, the passenger in that plane."

"I'm sorry for your loss."

"Don't say that. You don't know that."

"Ma'am it was rated as non-survivable. It's a recovery operation, not a rescue operation."

"Okay, forget that. Think what you want, but you don't know Cliff like I do. I just called to let you know I'm here at the airport in Las Vegas, Clyburn Executive Airport it's called, and I can provide any information on Knowles that you may need. I can be there tomorrow if you think I can help."

"We do have some volunteers, but unless you're an experienced mountain rescue team member somewhere, we don't want you."

"Okay, fine. Look, there's something else. You need to look for signs of sabotage. We think the plane was sabotaged."

"Sabotage? That's the first I've heard anything about that. What makes you think there was sabotage?"

"The pilot and passenger were the only two witnesses in a murder case who can authenticate a key piece of evidence, a confession from a co-conspirator. The defendant's lawyer arranged to get them both on a small plane rather than an airliner. Then the plane went down before they could do so. The details aren't important, but the D.A. agrees with me. You can call her if you don't believe me. Melissa Ingram, Clark County District Attorney's office."

"The victims were witnesses to a murder?"

"No, they're both retired law enforcement. They're the good guys. Like you and my husband. He's a cop. You know, protect and serve. They witnessed the confession, not the murder." Maeva knew that even though police and other law enforcement personnel were supposed to treat everyone equally under the law, they always cared a lot more for their comrades-in-arms. She was sucking up shamelessly, but whatever worked.

"Oh. I didn't know that. We were just told it was the burned out carcass of a small plane crash and to expect two bodies."

Maeva could hear Forster talking to someone in the background and the background buzz kicked up a notch in volume. This was apparently information of interest at the station.

He continued. "That's good you told me. We need an NTSB investigator there if we're looking for that. It was just a routine crash and the team doesn't have experts like that. We're just going in to recover bodies. The feds usually come in days or weeks later to determine cause. If we'd known it was an active crime scene, we could have gotten one here overnight. I'll try to make that happen. Give me your contact information."

Maeva did so. "Do you need the name and number of Cliff's wife? I'm in touch with her. She's law enforcement, too."

"No, we have the family contact information. Thank you, Maeva." So now that she was part of the law enforcement family, she qualified for first-name treatment instead of 'ma'am'.

Maeva felt a grudging sort of satisfaction when the call was over. At least she'd done something. It was frustrating feeling helpless. Perhaps getting the NTSB investigator there sooner will make a difference, she thought, but at best that could only lead to eventual prosecution. It wasn't going to bring Cliff back.

She took another look at the names on her list. The name Duc Bui stood out to her because it was one of two Vietnamese names and because his position was listed as mechanic, someone in a position to sabotage an aircraft. She asked around to see if he would talk to her, but found out he had gone home for the day. The only other Vietnamese name on the list was Robin Nguyen.

Maeva caught up with Robin at the car rental desk. She covered both the Hertz and Enterprise reservations at one desk. Maeva surmised that there was insufficient business at that airport to warrant two employees, so the companies partnered up. There were no customers at the desk.

Robin was the only one here now. She wore an unflattering company uniform consisting of a white long-sleeved dress shirt and black vest with a name tag sitting askew. Maeva's experience with hair and nail parlors in the San Jose area, nearly all manned by Southeast Asian women, had conditioned her to expect piercings or at least some extreme makeup and garish nails. She found none of that. Robin's makeup was tasteful and her nails bore clear polish, unusual for a late-20's-ish Vietnamese woman in Maeva's experience. Robin turned out to be bored and more than happy to talk to her.

Maeva explained to Robin that she was there to help find her partner who had been in the missing plane. Robin said the usual things about how terrible it was and how she hoped they were found safe. She remembered the pilot, Mr. Crosby, renting a car on Thursday. He was a regular at that airport and he was always nice, she said. She hadn't been on duty when he returned it Friday morning because she works the late shift.

Maeva asked if she remembered the man who was with Crosby that day on Thursday. She said she had a memory that someone was with him, but he had stood away from the desk and it wasn't anyone she recognized. She apologized for not really remembering him. Maeva hoped that by humanizing the victims, she might stir some extra motivation in Nguyen.

Robin was talkative and began talking about some of the other employees. They'd been speculating about how the missing plane might affect the airport's reputation. She mentioned the rumors about bad aviation gas, or the fears that pilots would blame their gas and stop coming. She said they'd been testing it. This was exactly the sort of thing Maeva wanted to hear, so she let Robin go on without asking questions.

Then it occurred to her that Robin was a bird's name just as Raven was. She looked at Robin's left hand. She wore a wedding ring, meaning Nguyen might be a married name. Could she be Tran's sister?

"I really like your name," Maeva commented when a break in the gossip stream gave her a chance. "I like birds. I had a friend named Raven and I always thought that was a cool name."

"That was my sister's name!" Robin squealed.

"Was?"

"Oh, she died. She got in with a bad crowd."

"Oh, I'm sorry."

"You couldn't know. Anyway, my mother loved birds, too. My brother's named Jay."

"Cool. Hey, I saw a guy listed here named Duck, too. This seems awfully appropriate for an airport. Employees with bird names."

"Oh, yeah. Duc." She pronounced it like Duke. "It's without the K. It's actually a common Vietnamese name, not related to the bird. He doesn't like to be called Duck, which is how everyone says it, so he uses Doug.

"Is he the one testing the gasoline? Maybe I should talk to him. Do you know him?"

Robin rolled her eyes. "Yeah, I know him." There was a short silence.

"You don't seem to hold him in high regard."

"Oh, he's okay. He's kind of a jerk sometimes, but I'm sure he'll help you if he can. Don't be surprised if he hits on you."

"I'm married."

"That won't stop him. You're pretty. That's enough to qualify."

Maeva showed no visible reaction, but the compliment felt good, especially coming from a woman who was obviously not trying to get in her pants. A horny man would compliment a warthog in a dress.

"Okay, thanks for the warning. Was Raven older than you?" Maeva wanted confirmation it was the right Raven.

"Yeah. We were five years apart."

The conversation continued for several more minutes, but Maeva learned nothing more that she could use. Robin must be Raven Tran's sister, which made her a prime suspect for being the gang contact here, but she seemed too nice and voluble to Maeva to raise her suspicions. She didn't have the access or skill set of a mechanic, either. Bui had those, but so did three other mechanics or techs who worked there, not to mention the dozens of private pilots who probably did, too.

She began to move toward the hangar area, but a tall security guard stopped her and asked where she was headed. She identified herself and explained that she was the partner of one of the men in the missing plane. The guard wore a uniform, but it wasn't TSA. General Aviation airports don't have TSA screeners, but they do have security, often much better than large commercial airports.

The guard was a beefy young man with Irish coloring and an arm tattoo that just peeked out from under his long-sleeved shirt. He probably wasn't allowed to have visible ones. One eyelid had a slight droop, which gave him a vaguely sinister look, but he kept a respectful demeanor and spoke well.

He told her he was sorry for her loss, a phrase she was getting sick of hearing, then told her she couldn't go back in the hangar area. She thought about challenging him, but realized it was a losing battle. She questioned him about the period from Thursday evening after Crosby's plane landed until Friday morning when it left. She learned that visiting pilots park on the ramp, out where the planes are accessible to any mechanic, airport employee, or private pilot who has regular access there. He also assured her that no one at the airport could have sabotaged the plane. He became quite agitated at the suggestion.

"It was pilot error. It always is. We run a tight ship here."

"I didn't mean anything by it. I didn't say it was sabotage. I just asked if someone could have accidentally or intentionally done something to the plane overnight. There must be mechanics or people who man the fuel pumps."

"Private pilots pump their own gas and pay by credit card like at a gas station. The mechanics are independent contractors. They usually keep regular hours, but they don't have to. Some work late. But there are security cameras covering the ramp area. And it's lighted. No one could do that undetected."

"So you've reviewed the security tape?"

"What? No! Of course not. Why would I? There's never been any suggestion of tampering."

"I'm suggesting it. So let's review it now."

"I don't have the authority. You'd have to get that from the head of security or the General Manager, Mr. Pasquali. There's no investigation underway and there won't be unless the accident is connected to something that happened here. Friends of passengers don't get to just come in and start investigating."

"I'm an investigator. I investigate." She flashed her private investigator license. She dug out a gold badge, too, and flashed that. It wasn't anything official, just something Cliff had made for her, but it counted as much as the private security guard uniform the man wore. "I'm not just a 'friend of a passenger.' I'm a professional like you." She used air quotes. "And I guarantee there is an investigation underway or very soon will be. The NTSB is being called to send an investigator overnight and they've been alerted to look for sabotage. They'll probably join the ground team going to the crash site in the morning."

"Wh-- …I haven't heard anything like that." He started to wag a finger at her, but then thought better of it. "Okay, that's new information. My boss needs to know that. I'm going into the security office now to let her know. But you can't go into the hangar area. I need you to stay right here."

"Fine. I'll stay here."

"And you still have no official capacity here. You can't see the footage." With that he left the lobby area and disappeared into a hallway.

Maeva sat in the small passenger waiting area and called Ellen. She updated her on what she had learned. Ellen thanked her but had no requests or suggestions. She was obviously very nervous and not-so-politely hurried Maeva off the conversation to keep her phone free for the search team. By the time she'd hung up, the guard was back.

"Okay, I told my boss about what you said. The recording is digital and stored on a server, but she said she'd download a copy onto an external drive and keep that in the safe as a backup. If someone is tampering with a plane, then they might be able to tamper with the security footage."

"Is she reviewing it?"

"No, it's hours long. That's the job of the NTSB if they deem it necessary. She's going home now. It's late."

Maeva hadn't really been paying attention to the time, but she realized it was approaching dark and she hadn't made any hotel reservations or had lunch or dinner. She'd been going at it all day long. As soon as she thought of it, hunger pains began to gnaw at her midsection. She left the airport to find food and a place to sleep.

Chapter 11

Monday morning

The day began as a clone of the previous day. Cliff arose, checked the waterholes, added two jiggers of mudwater to his hoard, and took care of his toilet needs. There was no food, so there was nothing to do but start down the streambed. He was still very thirsty even after the small water allotment he'd downed. In addition to the thirst and hunger and altitude sickness, he hadn't had any coffee for three days. He had the world's worst headache from the caffeine withdrawal and lack of oxygen.

The strap of his bindle was beginning to cut into his shoulders. He'd switched it from left to right regularly as he hiked along, but by now sore spots had developed on both sides. He took time to refashion the strap to go around his midsection. He'd used his necktie, the one he'd put on for court, to lengthen the strap so that it could be tied around his considerable midsection. The weight mostly rested on top of his geocaching pack, which already strapped around his hips.

This arrangement not only relieved the shoulder pain, it freed his hands. He'd been holding the strap with one hand as he hiked, but now with two hands, he could more easily climb over rocks and push aside the thick shriveled shrubbery that often blocked his way.

At least he had woken early this morning so he could hike with daylight and cool temperatures. Despite feeling weak and dehydrated, he was making the best time he had since the crash.

The streambed made a sharp turn to his right. He followed it around until he could see it broadening. He was no longer in a canyon but more of a valley. There was another canyon ahead to the north, but he ignored that and headed east down toward the valley. He could also see green tree growth a mile or two ahead. The ground sloped downward fairly sharply. Before he could get there, though, he had a formidable slog through and over more burn debris that had accumulated at the bend. The hillside was shallow enough here to allow him to climb up and past the blockage without having to climb all the way back to the ridgeline.

It took him over an hour, but he made it to the copse of greenery he'd spotted. Here he was able to see why the trees were still green. Another stream flowed down from the north. It was only a trickle, like the output when his kids didn't turn the bath faucet off all the way, but it was flowing water, good clean snow melt. He found a spot where the water dropped over a six-inch gap and settled in. As thirsty as he was, he didn't drink immediately. He filled his bottle halfway, put the cap on, and shook it, then dumped the water out. He knew there were contaminants in the bottle and a good rinse was a sensible precaution. He repeated the process for a second rinse; only then did he allow himself to drink. The effect was instant. His energy level skyrocketed and his mental fog lifted. He refilled the bottle all the way and drank that.

Now what? He began to cry. This caught him off guard. He wasn't a crier normally. But he realized now how much he had feared dying out here in this forbidding environment. Water meant survival, but for how long? He needed food, and he needed rescuing. He'd traveled at least five miles, although not in a straight line. He was at least three miles from the plane.

He turned on his GPS unit again. The valley was open enough that he obtained a good satellite lock within a minute. He'd marked the location of the crash so he could now determine the crash's distance and direction from his current position. It was 3.9 miles south southeast of his position. It was also at a higher elevation. There was no way he was going back there. His water wouldn't last, nor would his body.

He was now at 8,940 feet elevation. He'd come down over two thousand feet from the last time he'd measured. He thought about his lack of food. The hunger pangs were still there, but more of a dull background ache, not so pressing. His metabolism must have adjusted to the lack of food and started burning his fat supplies. Fortunately he had quite a substantial supply. He knew this couldn't go on much longer. He was noticeably weaker and it would get worse if he didn't find food soon.

The headache was getting better now. He must be almost over the caffeine withdrawal and the lower elevation was giving him more oxygen. But the water he'd drunk was causing pains in his abdomen. He didn't throw up, but he didn't dare try to drink any more. He curled up and waited for the pain to subside.

Duc Bui tried the location sharing app on his phone for the thirtieth time without luck. This did not surprise him. The burner phone in the plane's first aid kit had been fully charged Friday and left on, but its battery would have run down by now and was certainly out of cell phone range. It had most likely been destroyed in the crash, but if someone had survived, they probably would have taken the first aid kit and found the phone. If they had any sense, they'd turn it off to save the battery for when they reached cell phone coverage. He'd set the app to notify him with a push notification if it came on in a new location.

He'd had to drive five hours last night to get to June Lake, the town where the search team was convening. It was essential he join the search party. The search was being led by Mono County Search and Rescue, a team comprised of volunteers, but led by the Sheriff's Department. Bui was a city boy, not a mountain type, but he'd show up and demand to join the effort. If they didn't let him, he'd follow them. He had the plane's coordinates, too, so there's not really anything they could do about it. The main thing was to get to the plane and remove the cork in the fuel line. He knew from his planning and reading that it was an effective method of sabotage, but that the cork did not burn during a fire. The cork is protected by the fuel line.

He left his room and walked to the lobby of the motel. Several people were gathered there talking about the plans to go up into the mountains. They were obviously part of the search team. He grabbed a cup of coffee and a complimentary donut from the table. No one seemed to notice him. After a bit, he approached a pair of men talking about the crash. The taller one was older, with a gray grizzled full beard trimmed short. They both wore long-sleeved bright red pullover shirts and matching baseball caps. The shorter one was muscular and Asian.

"Hi. You guys on the search team?"

"Yeah," The older man said. He gave Bui an appraising look.

"I'm Doug from Clark County. I work at the airport where the plane took off. I'm going to join you on the search if you don't mind. I've been sent to collect evidence."

"Are you trained in mountain work?" the Asian guy asked.

"Not really, but I can let you guys do the hard part and blaze the trail for me. I don't intend to get in your way. I just need to take a fuel sample."

"The CAP said the plane was burned up." The older man spoke this time. They were tag teaming him.

"There's always some fuel left in the fuel lines. Even a couple of cc's will do for the test. There's been speculation our fuel was to blame. We need to determine if that's true."

"The NTSB sent someone. That woman over there. She can do that." Asian man again.

Bui looked out the window where the man had indicated and in the parking lot was a thickly built graying woman sporting an official-looking jacket of some kind with a patch on the shoulder. She was talking with another woman, a tall, dark-haired, slim, athletic type in the red outfit the men wore. The older woman's hair was cut in a butch. Her outdoor garb was well worn and she looked like she could pick him up and throw him across the parking lot.

"That's fine, she can get whatever samples she wants. I just need one for us."

"Where are your boots?" The older man was the speaker. Bui was getting tired of the back and forth, like watching a tennis match. He looked down at his feet. He was wearing Nike running shoes.

"They're in my room. I'll change before we go."

"No, you won't. Go, that is. Not with us," graybeard said. I'm sorry, but you're not qualified. We work as a team. We're volunteers, but you have to go through training and qualify in mountaineering and emergency first aid. There's an application process."

"The NTSB lady hasn't qualified with you."

"She has legal authority. You don't. We can't stop her. Besides, she's done this kind of work and has the training. She was chosen by the NTSB for this one for just that reason."

That told him what he needed to know. The men really couldn't stop anybody. It was a free country. He could pretend to acquiesce and then just follow the gang. "Alright, have it your way." He turned and went to the vending machine against the wall. He bought three bottles of water and a candy bar and returned to his room. He put the water in his backpack and gathered up everything. He'd prepaid for the room, so he was ready to leave as soon as the team did. He charged up his phone while he waited.

Fifteen minutes later the team members started piling in pickups and SUVs. He grabbed the phone and charger, shoved them in his pack and watched through the window as they headed onto the highway. Before the last one had left, he was in his car and backing out. He waited just long enough so he thought the last car wasn't watching him, then pulled onto the highway behind them with a gap of about fifty yards. There was no other traffic on the road.

The caravan pulled out onto June Lake Loop Road. Within a mile they reached a ski area. There was no snow here this time of year, but a ski area would have trails leading up the mountain and be easier hiking than open country. By his judgment the plane was about eight miles away to the southwest with an eleven thousand foot-high ridge between it and his position. This wasn't going to be easy.

He turned onto the road and drove slowly to allow the gap between him and the team to widen. He figured that there was only one place to go at the end, and that would be the ski area facilities. He'd let them get organized there and set off. He didn't need to organize anything so he'd pull in and park just as they were leaving, then follow them.

It happened exactly as he'd planned. He'd parked on the side of the road and watched from a hundred yards away as the team piled out of their various vehicles, loaded on packs and gear, and finally set off on foot. No one noticed him. He drove into the parking lot and parked next to their vehicles. His tricked-up Mustang looked out of place next to the Suburbans and F-150s, but he didn't care. He checked his phone. There was a good signal here, but nothing from the burner phone.

He got out of his car, slung his backpack over his shoulders, and set off after them. They were halfway up the main ski run before anyone noticed him two hundred yards behind. The group stopped. The grey-haired man yelled at him go back. Bui kept walking.

When he reached the group, greybeard, now obvious as the leader, unleashed a tirade on him, but it did no good. Bui apologized, but promised to stay out of everybody's way and said not to mind him. After a few minutes of arguing and frustration, the leader said they might as well let him come along. If he got in trouble going it alone, the team would just have to rescue him anyway. Better to keep him close so they could keep him safe. Soon the whole assembly, Bui included, was on its way up the mountain.

Once he could stand, Cliff took another drink, but very slowly. He felt refreshed once more. His headache was almost totally gone. He was tempted to set up camp here. Maybe he could shoot an animal for food and stay until he was rescued. But he realized that no one would be looking here. He was too far from the plane. He hadn't heard any planes or helicopters. He had to get out on his own.

He refilled his water bottle and reassessed what he was carrying. He took out his book and the spare ammo magazine. He'd leave them here. The weight just wasn't worth it. He decided to leave them behind. His geocaching bag included a Leatherman folding knife. That was possibly more useful and not as heavy. He decided to keep that. That knife was one of the reasons he'd wanted to fly with Jim. He couldn't take it on an airline with just his carryon bag. He'd had one knife confiscated before at the security line when he'd forgotten it was in his bag. If he was going geocaching on a trip, he had to put it in checked luggage which always delayed things. He knew that Jim flew his own plane largely for the same reason, so he could take his gun. Cliff decided to keep all the clothing. Most of it was light and now that he'd fashioned the bindle around his waist instead of over his shoulder, it was easier to carry. He'd need layers for nighttime warmth.

Once he settled on what he could carry, he set off downstream again. After an hour he stopped to rest. Through a gap in the terrain he could see miles to the east from this point. There were groves of trees, evergreens, not blackened skeletons, miles in the distance. He saw no signs of civilization, no telephone or power wires, no roads or buildings. There were still mountains to either side and behind him, but this gap gave him an incentive to try the cell phone. Maybe the signal could make it through that gap and connect with a tower somewhere out there.

He pulled Jim's emergency phone from his pocket and pressed the power button. The screen came to life, but showed nothing besides the time against a black background. He touched the screen and it asked for a PIN, but there was also a red icon for emergency calling. He ignored the PIN and pressed the icon to call 911. The screen lit up but no sound of dialing or ringing came from the device. The word "dialing" appeared. After what seemed like an eternity the word "connecting" appeared, but there was still no sound. It was at that point he noticed the tiny icons in the top corner. The battery icon showed about a quarter of its juice was left. But the fan-shaped one that indicated signal strength showed zero.

The word "connecting" stayed on the screen for a full minute with no further sign it had connected. He tried saying hello into the phone several times, but he may as well have been talking to a rock. He turned it off, replaced it in his pocket, and resumed his downward trek. He continued for three or four hours. The heat was becoming even more brutal.

The stream here presented another convenient spot to refill his water bottle, so he took another long drink and refilled. As he sat resting on a boulder, he noticed something on the ground a few feet up the hill – a snake. It wasn't moving. He crept closer. It wasn't a rattler, that much he could tell. Rattlesnakes were common in the Sierras and Coast range where he usually geocached; he knew he'd recognize one. He thought it was a kingsnake, but right now he was thinking more snake ala king.

He quietly withdrew his gun and leveled it at the snake. The snake was sunning itself and paid no attention. Cliff pulled the trigger. The report startled him, even though he'd expected it. He'd forgotten how loud gunshots were. At firearms training he'd always worn mandatory ear protection. The snake had an obvious wound, but it was now thrashing around. It was a big snake and the shot hadn't killed it. Cliff was never a great shot and had aimed at the center of mass to be sure of hitting it. Now he wished he'd aimed for the head. A hole mid-body wasn't fatal.

He took aim at the head for a second shot, but the snake wasn't cooperating. Its head was thrashing more than any other part. Suddenly it started to slither away between two large rocks. Cliff couldn't let it get away, so he shot again. The second shot missed altogether. He shot once more and the snake performed a final spectacular acrobatic death throe and lay dead.

Cliff was sweating profusely from the tension and the heat. He leaned over to pull the snake's body free, but as he did so, his glasses, lubricated by his perspiration, slipped off his head. His autonomic reaction shot his hand out to grab them midair, but instead of grasping them, he accidentally batted them downward and to the left. He saw only a blur as they flew between two boulders lining the creek, one of them the boulder he had just been sitting on.

His vision was horrible without his glasses. His very survival depended on retrieving them. He scrambled down to where he'd seen them disappear and tried to reach them. He wasn't even sure he was reaching into the right spot. It was dark between the boulders and the space was narrow. He could only fumble blindly and only a few inches. His hand was too big to reach farther. He could only get the fingers of one hand in the slot.

His middle finger touched the slick plastic arm of what must be his glasses' temple piece. He could feel the glasses slip another millimeter or two down. He couldn't get his thumb and finger together in the opening so he took another approach. He made a wide V shape with his index and middle fingers and snapped them together. Success! He could feel the plastic between them, the pad of his middle finger pressing it against the nail of his index finger. He tried to pull the glasses out, but it was immediately clear that they were stuck.

He managed to keep his grip, slight though it was. He knew that if he pulled too hard, he'd lose it and the glasses would likely slip down completely out of reach. In a painstakingly slow process, he rocked the glasses back and forth until they moved up an inch. He could feel and hear the scratching of the lens against the rock. Eventually he raised them enough so that he could get his thumb on the plastic piece. He could tell from the curvature that he was holding the part that went over the ear.

Now he could pinch hard enough so that he wouldn't lose his grip if he met resistance. He had to pull; there was no other option. He knew he might scratch the lenses, but they would still restore his vision. He gradually increased the force until he felt the glasses move, but they wedged in tightly again and stopped. They were higher up now. He maneuvered his thumb and finger farther down the stem until he was closer to the lens. Gripping tighter than before he pulled harder. There was a snap and he almost fell back from the sudden release of pressure. He held in his hand the broken temple piece. It had broken off right at the hinge. He immediately thought of Thanksgiving dinner as a kid when he always lost the wishbone pull to his sister. He shook off the thought.

He looked into the space between the rocks and saw nothing but black. His heart sank for a moment, but he realized his vision was so bad he wouldn't have been able to make them out in the darkness even if they hadn't moved. Gingerly he felt in the crack with his fingers once more. The glasses hadn't moved. They were now high enough up that Cliff could get his thumb and forefinger on the frame around one lens.

He pulled gently, but the glasses didn't move. Wiggling them back and forth did nothing. It was time to resolve this while he still had a good grip. He yanked as hard as he could and heard another crack as the glasses came free. He held the frame up with one hand and inspected the glasses by feel with his other. The other temple piece had broken off and the frame was broken. Worse, one lens had fallen out. The second one was in the frame, but slipped out as he felt it. It fell at his feet. The clear lens was virtually invisible to him but it had fallen directly at his feet. He squatted and felt around until he found it.

The frame was a total loss. With both temples gone and the frame cracked, it wouldn't hold a lens. But at least he had one lens. He held that up to his right eye. It helped, but didn't seem right. He held it up to his left eye and suddenly the world became clear. His two eyes didn't have the same prescription; this was obviously the left lens. His whole body shook with relief. It would be awkward, but he could use the lens. He was no longer practically blind.

He pocketed the lens, checking to make sure there was no hole in the pocket, and went back up to where the snake lay dead. He pulled the body out from its spot. He still hadn't hit the head, but his third shot had severed the spine just behind the head. It was time to put that Leatherman to use. Slicing the snake open and extracting the meat wasn't as difficult as he'd expected, but it took time. It came off in long strips and was white like chicken. He had no way to cook it, so he bit off a raw chunk. He began to chew it, but it was tough like any raw meat, so he swallowed it in whole chunks.

His stomach immediately reacted. It clenched up and launched a startling cacophony of gastronomic noises. Cliff remained still until he knew whether his stomach would accept the offering. There were a couple of times when he thought it might come back up, but after twenty minutes, he was confident the drama was over.

He laid out the other strips of meat on a boulder and found a smaller rock to use as a mallet. He pounded the meat as flat as he could and left it in the sun to dry. Snake jerky would serve him well, he thought.

They'd been hiking for almost two hours. The first half hour had been up the ski slope. The terrain there wasn't difficult, but it was steep. Once they'd gotten above the top of the ski area, the way had become harder to pass through. So this was what bushwhacking meant, Bui thought. It wasn't fun.

His phone made a beep. He must still be in range of the cell service at the Loop Road. He looked at the notification page. The emergency cell phone he stashed in the plane had been detected in a new location! It couldn't have been found by searchers. He was with the search crew and they were miles away. He pressed the icon to save the phone's location as latitude and longitude numbers. Then he checked that against the coordinates the Civil Air Patrol had given them of the plane's wreckage. They didn't match! The phone was on and several miles from the plane. That could mean only one thing: someone had survived and was carrying the phone. It was too far away to have been thrown from the plane during the crash. The survivor must be trying to call for a rescue.

The screen changed. The saved coordinates still appeared, but now the turning icon indicated that it was searching for the location of the other phone. After a minute, a message appeared stating that the target phone was not detected. That was both good news and bad news. The phone must have lost signal and therefore couldn't be used to call 911. The bad news was that Bui wouldn't know of any further movement or its direction.

He enlarged the map and did some rough calculations. The search team was heading in more or less a straight line to the crash site. The survivor was well north and east of the plane. He was moving generally toward them, but probably not in a straight line. He might be following terrain rather than a specific planned route. If he continued to do that, it looked like he would cross the path of the team, but ahead of them, moving in an eastward direction and eventually hit Highway 395.

"Hey, Doug! What's the hold-up?" Greybeard was yelling at him. The group had moved ahead by quite a bit while he was looking at his phone.

"Sorry."

"Put the phone away. If you can't keep up, go back down."

"I can keep up." He pocketed the phone. He didn't know how much longer he'd have cell service but he had to keep it on now. He scurried up the hill and rejoined the group to a chorus of hoots and sarcastic jibes.

Forty minutes later his phone pinged again. The signal strength indicator was almost at zero. This would probably be the last point where he would have cell service. He checked the app. The survivor was now farther north. Bui could now determine his direction of travel. He was heading northeast instead of due east. Instead of Highway 395, he'd hit the June Lake Loop Road, which was closer. He was no longer following terrain; instead he was taking the shortest route to civilization. Bui wondered whether both men had survived. It could be survivors plural, but he doubted it. That would make his job more difficult.

Like the last time, the signal on the other end dropped off quickly and the app lost the location. He couldn't tell whether the survivor had been able to call 911 and report his location. He figured that if he had done so, the search team would be notified. Several of them had radios which presumably could receive in this terrain.

Without a proper map and tools he could only estimate, but now with the new route, Bui figured the survivor, or survivors, would cross their path about a half mile ahead of where the rescue team was now, but it would take at least three hours, assuming the survivor continued at his current speed and direction. The search team would be well ahead by that time, almost to the crash site.

He had a decision to make. Should he stick with the group and try to get the cork in the plugged line out, or should he try to intercept the survivor and take care of him once and for all? The decision wasn't difficult. If the survivor made it to civilization, he'd be under protection and the recording would be put in evidence. The game would be up. The NTSB investigator might very well miss the cork. None of the others would be looking for that. They were just there to haul out the bodies. Even if the cork was found, they couldn't trace that to him. He had to go for the survivor and silence him. He would stick with the group for another half mile and stop at the approximate point the survivor would cross. He'd make up an excuse to stay there.

"Doug! Move it!"

"Coming."

Now that he had food and water, meager though it was, Cliff felt certain he could get to civilization on his own. He had a better idea of the terrain now. If he continued to follow the streambed, he'd go almost due east and reach 395. But he doubted he could make it today. He'd have to sleep outdoors again and might not find another water source. The visible water flow had disappeared, probably evaporating into the air. On the GPS map he could see a closer road, the June Lake Loop to the north. It would require going up and over two ridges in full sunlight and 100° temperatures, but he should reach the road today around sunset. The town of June Lake lay at the end of the road.

He tried calling 911 again. This time it rang. Someone picked up on the other end, a woman.

"What is your emergency?"

"I'm in the mountains and need food and medical attention."

"What is your location?"

The phone went dead. He looked at the screen and realized the battery was drained. He'd forgotten to turn it off after the last call. When a cell phone doesn't have a good signal, it keeps boosting the power trying to reach a tower. This drains the battery at an accelerated rate when there is no tower nearby. Damn!

He kicked himself for not leading with his identity and location. The initial question from the 911 operator "what is your emergency?" was standard, but it was useless in this case. He realized that based on his response he could be any random hiker anywhere in California or Nevada. He had no idea what jurisdiction answered the call. It's often the Highway Patrol in California and they may be hundreds of miles away, but in towns or cities the local police or sheriff's office usually answers.

They would have a record of the telephone number he called from, but it was the phone in the first aid kit. He assumed that would come back to Jim. Then they'd know it was one of the survivors of the plane crash. They must at least have a general idea of the location by now. But how long would it take to trace it? It wasn't a brand name phone. At least he couldn't tell if it was from the exterior. It looked like one of those prepaid phones. Without the PIN he couldn't unlock it so he couldn't see the brand or use the apps on it. Did it have a GPS feature? He didn't know if the 911 operator had been able to capture his location somehow from that brief call. He decided he couldn't stay where he was. He would go north over the ridges and try to make the road by nightfall.

Chapter 12

The timing worked out well for Bui. The group reached the base of the first steep ridge at almost the exact point he believed the survivor would cross their path. He called to the leader greybeard, whose real name he'd learned was Darryl, that he couldn't handle the rock climbing they faced and said he'd head back down.

"Are you sure you can make it back?" The tone of his voice left no doubt he was relieved to be rid of Bui, but he'd felt compelled to ask.

"Of course."

"Okay, then. We'll radio when we get to the plane. If you give me your phone number I can have the sheriff call you. If you have any questions about the condition of the plane or passengers, you can relay those through dispatch and we can try to answer them."

The NTSB woman jumped into the conversation. "Doug, if you give me your sample container, I can collect a fuel sample for you."

Bui wasn't prepared for this. His story about collecting a fuel sample had been a bluff, an improvisation to justify his tagging along. The search team had taken him at his word and assumed he was heading back down to the ski area or back to June Lake where he would be in cell phone range. In reality, he would be waiting right in this spot for the survivor to come by. There was no cell coverage here. It might seem suspicious if his phone wasn't on the grid.

"No, that's alright. I've decided I don't need it. I hadn't realized there would be someone from the NTSB along when I first showed up. We'll rely on your findings of the cause. I'm sure our av fuel is good. No one else has had any trouble with it. It was probably pilot error. I wouldn't bother checking the fuel if I were you." He didn't want her to check the fuel lines. She might find the cork. He'd hoped to get to them before she did. At least he knew she wouldn't find the cell phone. The survivor had that. He was concerned that she would discover he'd tampered with the fuel gauge, but there was nothing he could do about that.

The woman and several other members looked at him like he was nuts. He'd come all this way fighting the team and now it's "never mind?"

"Alright. Fine with me," the woman said.

"Are you going to come back this way?" Bui asked.

"No," Darryl said. "We're going to reconnoiter and find a spot near the wreck where a helicopter can lower a gurney. They couldn't see one from the air. The ravine's too deep and the walls too close together. The winds are tricky, too. A dangling harness could snag on the rocks. We'll haul the bodies up to the ridge top by rope and radio our coordinates. The helicopter will come in and pick them up and a couple of us with it. The rest will have to wait for the chopper to come back and get them afterward."

"Okay. Good plan. Thanks for letting me stay with you this far."

"Good luck, Doug."

Bui waved and headed back down the way they'd come just long enough to be out of sight behind some pine trees. As soon as the group was out of sight over the ridge, he'd move back.

Monday morning

Maeva called Melissa Ingram early. She knew that D.A.s often had court appearances at 8:30 or 9:00 and she wanted to catch her before that. Ingram picked up.

"Ingram."

"Melissa, it's Maeva. Have you heard anything?"

"No, have you?"

"No. Hey, I have a possible lead on one of the people involved in the case. That guy Duck you mentioned."

"Yeah? I'm listening."

"There's this guy at the airport where the plane took off – Clyburn. His name is Duc Bui. He's a mechanic. He's in a good position to sabotage a plane. He goes by Doug here, but apparently people sometimes call him Duck."

"His name hasn't come up in the case. I'd remember it."

"Get this. Raven Tran's sister works at that airport, too. She knows Bui and apparently doesn't much like him. I know that's not proof, but there is at least an indirect tie."

"Have you told detective Slonsky?"

"No, he never contacted me."

"Yeah, well, I'm afraid he's not my first choice for a lead investigator. He's due to retire in another six months and isn't shy about letting people know. He's trying to avoid doing anything that will drag him back in for a trial. He should be named Slowsky. But I can talk to his boss. I'll have the task force check him out. Hold on a second."

There was a pause while Maeva heard a series of keyboard taps on the other end. Ingram came back on the line.

"Okay, I pulled up the list of all the telephone contacts Truong had during the four-month investigation. None of them come back to a Duc Bui, although there are several unidentified numbers, probably burner phones. He's not on the list of gang members who've been identified at gang raves."

"Okay, it's just a suspicion. I could be wrong. But here's something else. I'm at the airport now. I got here early because I wanted to interview Bui. I tried to interview him yesterday and couldn't because he'd already left. So now I find out he's not here today. He told the manager that he was going up to join the search operation for the plane."

"Why? Is he some kind of Search and Rescue volunteer?"

"No, I don't think so. The manager said he's never gotten any indication of him being outdoorsy."

"They're calling it a recovery operation according to the news. Not search and rescue."

"Don't remind me. Look, just have your task force check him out."

"Okay, thanks, Maeva. Keep me informed. I have to get to court."

"Will do. Bye."

Maeva ended the call and immediately called Ellen. Maeva updated her on everything she'd learned, explaining the whole case and Cliff's role in it. Ellen became steely in her resolve to make someone pay if it turned out the plane was sabotaged. She was at home, needing to stay with the kids and stay ready to leave at a moment's notice if word came from the search team. Ellen told her that Melissa Ingram had called her to offer her condolences, something Ellen both resented and appreciated. Cliff was still alive, dammit. At least until they found a body.

As soon as she hung up, her phone rang. It was a local number, and she figured it was related to the case, so she answered.

"Maeva Hanssen."

"This is Detective Slonsky. The D.A. says I'm supposed to call you."

"You heard what happened to my boss and the other witness, Crosby?"

"Yeah, she filled me in. Tough break. I hope he's okay."

"So what do you know about Duc Bui?"

"Look, I don't know you. You're not part of the investigation and I can't share anything with you. I can tell you I've never heard of this Bui guy until Ingram mentioned him. That came from you, I guess. We'll check him out when we get a chance. I've got other cases that are higher priority right now."

"Can I meet with you?"

"No. You should just go home. This case is no place for a girl. No offense. That gang is a bunch of killers. If you're actually onto something, you're going to end up like Mendoza and Tran. I was ordered to call you and I have, but that's it. Take my advice. It's good advice. Go home. I gotta go. Goodbye."

The red Call Ended icon appeared on Maeva's phone. "Thanks for nothing, asshole," she said uselessly into the instrument.

By noon the search team had reached the entrance to the ravine where the plane had landed. The ravine was narrow and the stream bed that ran through it was dry and clogged with the burned-out skeletons of the trees that had been destroyed in the fires two years earlier.

Rather than trying to pick their way over the logjams and boulders, they decided to walk along the ridgeline until they were over the plane, and rappel down. It was the clearer, faster route. It took half an hour to get over the plane and another fifteen minutes to get the whole team down. They gathered about fifty feet from the plane.

The team was so sure there could be no survivors, the first ones down didn't even go over to the wreckage to see if anyone was alive. They had a rude awakening when they approached it as a group and someone gasped, "That's a body! He's been laid out."

The charred remains of Jim Crosby had been mistaken for an airplane part from a distance, but up close it was obvious not only that it was a man's form, but that it had been pulled from the plane and laid out neatly next to it. That meant the other soul, pilot or passenger, they didn't know which, must have survived. Immediately the team rushed around pulling apart the wreckage looking to be sure there wasn't a survivor sheltering in the fuselage. The NTSB representative began yelling at them not to disturb the scene, but no one paid attention to her.

Darryl got on the radio to try to let the sheriff's department know there was a survivor, but couldn't get through. The rock walls blocked the signal.

"Look at that." He pointed to a red-black splotch on a rock by the ravine wall. "That's blood. There's a survivor and he didn't go up these walls, not without climbing gear. Randy, you take Trish downstream and see if he's there. He'll need water, food, and probably first aid. I'll go back up the ropes to get a radio signal to the sheriff to let them know." He turned to the other two volunteers. "You stay here and help the NTSB. When I can I'll come back down to help with the body."

Randy Whiting had been born in Korea, but had been adopted by an American family as an infant. He didn't speak Korean or eat Korean food, but people often asked him if he was Chinese or Korean. He always said no, he was American. That shut them up. He was the best tracker in the group, although he was no expert. They hadn't formed the team with tracking in mind. Trish had also worked as a qualified paramedic, he knew, so it made sense to send her in case they found him injured.

He and Trish headed north along the same route Cliff had taken. They were younger than Cliff, more agile, experienced, better equipped, and knew the terrain. They also had Camelbaks of water. That all explained their pace, which was more than twice what Cliff's had been. They were eighty minutes along when Trish spotted the cairn.

"Randy, over here. Look."

"Is that new?"

"I'm sure of it. There's no trail here. I doubt anyone else has ever been here. He must have made it."

"But why?" Randy looked around. The way was relatively clear here. There was no reason to stop here that they could see. Nothing looked noteworthy. No water.

Trish began to disassemble the cairn to see if there was a note or something else in it that would provide a clue. She found nothing. "Which guy was it? The pilot?"

"I don't know. We didn't ID the body. Does it matter?"

"Not really. It just, well, I think it's a good sign. I heard the men weren't outdoorsmen. Someone knew enough to mark a path. He probably didn't have any tools or other methods, like slashing a tree. Maybe it means he could still be alive."

"Of course he could. It was the crash that was supposed to be non-survivable. Anyone who made it through that has a chance out here."

"It's been three days with ninety-odd degree highs and two percent humidity. And he was losing blood."

"He made it this far. Let's keep going."

They headed down at an accelerated pace, sometimes taking risky leaps from rock to rock, a real-life parkour, not some click-hungry poseur's heavily edited video. Ten minutes later they came to the same blockage that had rebuffed Cliff.

"Hold up, Randy. That's not passable."

"We can get by. Look on the right. If we tie off … "

"Okay, maybe *we* could, but think about it. Could *he*?"

He did think about it and it didn't take long for him to reach the same conclusion she had. He would have turned back. It was impossible to go up the canyon walls and the blockage obstructed both downstream and across the stream bed for anyone who wasn't fit and had rock climbing experience.

"The cairn. That's what it was for. He was trying to mark where he left the …" The right word failed him. He was about to say trail, but there was no trail.

"… bottom," Trish finished the sentence. "Yeah, he must have decided to go over the ridge there. It was a shallower slope there."

"Shit! We should have thought of that. C'mon, let's go back."

Their parkour in the reverse direction was even more reckless, if that was possible, but they both made it to the cairn safely. They took a break to drink water and rest.

"Damn it! I should have seen it," Randy hissed. "Look, that's a footprint." He tried to reach Darryl on the radio, but the signal wasn't clear enough. “Well, it’s all for the best. We have to let the others know and we’ll have to get up higher for that anyway.”

“Race you to the top.” Trish began scrambling up the side of the canyon. Proper boots and gloves made the climb quite manageable for a rockclimber acclimated to the oxygen level. Randy followed right behind.

At the top he had a clear radio signal. He could hear a tactical conversation going on between Darryl and the sheriff's office dispatch. He soon learned that a helicopter and pilot had now been appropriated for a rescue because of the discovery, but it was waiting for a spotter and preferably a location of the survivor before taking off. The team at the plane site had identified the body as that of the pilot. The survivor was the passenger, Cliff Knowles.

“This is Randy. We have a trail of sorts. He left a cairn to mark where he left the canyon and came over the ridge. He must have gone down the other side. He’s headed northeast, at least for a couple of miles. He’s probably going to follow White Creek until it joins Glass Creek. If he knows what he’s doing, he’ll end up at the meadow at the foot of the Obsidian Dome, but that’s just a guess. There’s no water here.”

“Good work. It gives us an idea where to search. As soon as the spotter gets here, we’re airborne.”

“We aren’t expert trackers and the ground here is mostly granite. Chances of finding a good trail are slim. We can head downstream until it opens up, but we can’t go all the way to June Mountain on a guess. He could go due north at the split or decide to go up top the ridge like he did right here.”

Darryl responded, “Understood. We don’t want to have to rescue you. If you don’t find him in the next hour, come back here to the crash site.”

“Roger.”

Randy and Trish began to make their way down the slope hopping between boulders like pachinko balls.

Chapter 13

The loss of his glasses meant he'd have to travel slower. He couldn't hold the one good lens up to his eye as he hiked. He needed both hands free for balance and for climbing over rocks or pushing aside foliage. The lens stayed in his pocket. The world was in soft focus, but he wasn't blind. He continued to stay close to the creek, sometimes even stepping in the water because he misjudged his footing. His shoes were totally ruined by now.

His head was clearer now both because the caffeine headache was gone and because he'd found water. So he could tell that he was getting weaker. A lizard and some snake jerky didn't come close to making a meal and he'd been using a lot of energy over the last three days. He'd scraped his leg more than once, opening up the wound from the plane crash. He was worried it would become infected, but seemed okay for now and wasn't bleeding.

As he came down the mountain, he reached a more wooded area, a mix of conifers and birches. This area had not been burned. The shade was welcome but the landscape here presented another challenge. The ground was covered in a layer of needles, pine cones, and leaves. Cliff had been walking on packed dirt and granite, solid footing, in other words. Here he couldn't see what was under the leaves and needles. The surface may look level, but it could hide holes, rocks and the spaces between. A hidden branch could snap under his weight. One bad step that twisted an ankle taught him he had to test every step before putting his weight on it. This would slow him even more.

He stopped to take a rest and think about his predicament. He no longer thought he could make the road by sundown. He'd have to spend another night in the open. The cold nights sucked energy from his body like a parasite.

As he sat on a small rise, he noticed a bird flitting between trees. Without his glasses he couldn't tell what kind it was, but it looked fairly big and plump to him. Maybe a jay. He pulled the lens from his pocket and took another look. Yes, it was a jay, and it was just sitting on a limb, fat and happy. Cliff was neither. Well, maybe just a little fat.

He pulled out the pistol and gave it a quick check. It was ready to fire. The lens was for his left eye, not his right. The prescription was different for the two sides. That meant he had to hold the lens to his left eye with his left hand and aim through that eye while shooting right-handed. In theory it shouldn't matter which eye was used to aim, but in practice, it did. It felt awkward. His FBI training did include some left-handed (or off-handed as it was known since lefties had to shoot right-handed) and left-eyed shooting, but it was only for a few rounds and he was never good at it. In fact, he was never good at firearms anyway.

His next meal depended on his marksmanship now, so he took careful aim. He held his breath and squeezed the trigger. The shot resonated through the woods and the jay flew away. A clean miss. Damn! He continued sitting still, hoping it would fly back.

The team had been out of sight for over an hour. Bui stayed at the foot of the scarp where he had left the team. The survivor should be coming through here any minute if he stayed on a straight line. There was no cell phone coverage here, so it was pointless to try to use the phone finder app.

It was the snap of a branch that first alerted him. A person or an animal had been moving through the brush somewhere in the vicinity. He listened intently while holding his breath. It was faint, but the sound reoccurred. It was to his right and downhill. He moved in the general direction of the sound, taking care not to make noise.

Then he heard the sound of someone clearing his throat. That was a human. Whoever it was, they weren't moving very quickly. Bui continued to move downhill on what he thought was an intercept path. He kept just outside the wooded area. He could move faster on the rocks and could see better. The person he was stalking was in the woods and the trees blocked a clear view. It was hard to judge distance without a direct sight line. He guessed maybe two hundred yards away.

This continued for ten minutes or so, and the distance was definitely closing. The sounds of snapping branches was louder. Bui pulled out the gun he'd concealed in his backpack. He checked it over and made it ready to fire. They could be coming face to face any second.

Then he heard it. A gunshot! And close. Really? The survivor was armed! He hadn't counted on that. He stopped short and realized he was sweating and shaking. He dropped to the ground. He wasn't sure if the shot had been aimed at him. He hadn't heard any nearby impact. Had the survivor heard him and shot the gun to draw his attention, to get rescued? Had anybody else heard the shot? These questions raced through his mind but no immediate answer.

He didn't know which of the two men was the survivor, but he knew they were retired FBI agents. They were probably crack shots. He'd seen the shows on television. They trained intensively. Bui had never shot anyone. The only time he'd shot his gun was blasting some cactus out in the desert. His Glock was modified for fully automatic fire. It had been fun blasting away, but he'd never done real target practice. Accuracy hadn't seemed all that important when you shot a spray of ten rounds. He wasn't part of the street gang; he was the logistics coordinator. Dice had intentionally insisted he keep isolated from the thugs. Getting in a shootout with an FBI agent didn't seem like a good idea.

The more he thought about it, the more he felt sure the shot had not been intended for him. How would the survivor know he was being hunted? It was more likely he was sensing that he was near civilization and was trying to attract attention. Taking a distant shot at a person would be risky. There was too much of a chance he'd miss. Mulling this over, he decided the best strategy would be to hail the survivor and see if he could approach. Once he got within a few feet, if the man didn't have a gun in his hand, he'd be an easy target.

Bui stood and listened for another minute. There was no more noise, no second shot. Taking the plunge he called out, "Hey! You there! Are you okay?" He began walking in the direction of the shot, entering the woods. "We're here to rescue you. Come on out."

Cliff heard a voice. He couldn't make out the words, but it was a human voice, a man's voice. He was near civilization. He was going to be saved! He called back. "Over here! I'm over here."

He couldn't hear any reply. His hearing was somewhat impaired by the shot. He figured that if he couldn't hear the other man, then that man probably couldn't hear him. The other person might be going off in the wrong direction. This could be his only chance. He decided to crank off another round. That would be heard for sure.

He started to shoot straight up in the air but hesitated, remembering that what goes up must come down. He knew of cases where a bullet falling back to earth had killed someone on the ground. He leveled the gun at the trees, but then remembered that ricochets off trees and rocks could also kill. He aimed, not, pointed, the gun at a forty-five degree angle over the treetops the opposite direction from where he thought the voice had been. Plugging one ear with his finger, he shot another round.

He thought about moving toward the voice, but he wasn't sure where it was and his twisted ankle made that difficult. More importantly, the other person might be heading to where he had shot. It didn't work if both parties were moving. One needed to stay still and the other could find him.

Bui heard the second shot and hesitated once again. He hadn't heard any voice response to his first call. He stepped behind a tree and waited. He still wasn't sure if the man was trying to shoot him or call for help.

"Don't shoot! I'm here to help. Where are you?"

This time he heard a man's voice in response. "Over here. I'm over here. I need help." It was muffled by the thick woods, but he caught enough of it to be able to know the man was trying to attract him.

"Keep talking. I'll follow your voice."

The man continued calling out "Here, I'm over here."

Bui kept moving that direction. He put his Glock in his waistband in the small of his back. He could draw it quickly when the time came, but he kept one hand on the butt for now. He wanted to see the FBI agent with no gun in his hand before showing up with empty hands himself.

He caught a glimpse of the man now between the trees. He watched as the man stood. He'd been sitting. He was cocking his head this way and that, trying to locate where Bui was from the sound. He had some kind of weird wrap around his head. His hands were empty.

"I see you. I'm coming," Bui called. He took his hand from the butt of the gun and stood straight. He tried to present a friendly aspect – a smile, a wave. He stepped forward through the trees. The man turned and saw him and broke into a big smile. The man waved.

Cliff saw the man approaching. Thank God. Finally, a rescue. His bindle was already off his shoulder and situated on the rock. He placed his gun on top of it, making sure it was stable and not going to slip off and fall. He stood up, raised his hand and waved with his right hand while reaching in his left pocket with his other hand.

The rescuer reached a point about twenty feet away smiling back at him, returning the wave. Cliff brought the lens to his left eye. The blurry figure came into focus. Something clicked. Something was off. Cliff was a master of deduction, but this wasn't deduction. There was no logical process going, no adding up the clues. It was pure instinct.

The rescuer just didn't look right. He didn't act right. He wasn't dressed right. Ordinary Nikes out here? The backpack was a kid's backpack, not a hiker's. He wore an ordinary baseball cap, not a hat with a large brim or neck covering. The sun was brutal out here at this elevation and anyone looking for him would be prepared. The man looked Vietnamese, the same as the defendant in the case. Perhaps under other circumstances, reading a crime novel or watching a movie maybe, he could have recognized these as clues and made the leap.

That's not what happened. There wasn't time for that. He took that all in but any processing was subconscious. What triggered instant recognition of danger was the man's right hand. It had been waving, but now was reaching behind his back at waist level, below the backpack: where a gang banger would stash a gun for a quick draw. Cliff turned and reached for his own gun. Cliff's hand closed on the gun's grip.

Two shots rang out.

Chapter 14

Maeva paced around the airport lobby. She wasn't comfortable with Duc Bui disappearing right after she'd made the connection with the case. It was a weak connection, for sure. Duc, or Doug as he liked to be called, may or may not be the Duck who was present at the murder. But Bui knew Robin Tran, and Robin's sister Raven was Truong's girlfriend. Deceased girlfriend.

She went to the manager's office and knocked. His secretary was nowhere around. He could see Maeva through the glass. He wiped the expression off his face, but it was obvious he was becoming irritated at her theories and interruptions. He smiled and waved her in.

"Hi. I have a question. Did you send Doug Bui to join the search for the plane?"

"Uh, Miss …"

"Hanssen. Maeva Hanssen."

"Hanssen. You really should leave this investigation to the professionals."

"I am a professional."

"You know what I mean. Police, sheriffs. NTSB."

"Thank you for the advice," she said drily. "You haven't answered my question."

"No, I didn't send him. Why would I? I don't have the authority to send him anywhere. He's an independent contractor, not an employee. He rents space and charges the pilots. And if I was going to send someone, he'd be the last person I'd send. He's a mechanic. He's good with electronics. He plays video games and eats junk food. He's about as qualified to be doing search and rescue … or recovery … as I am to repair an altimeter."

"Don't you think it's odd that he went up there to join the search team?" She avoided the uncomfortable distinction between rescue and recovery.

"Okay, it's odd. So what?" His phone rang. "I have to take this." He picked up the phone without waiting for her to give him consent.

Maeva stood there while the manager launched into a lengthy conversation with a plane owner about hangar and tie down fees. There was some ongoing argument there which Maeva didn't care to listen to, so she left.

She took a seat in the lobby again and dialed the number she'd gotten from Deputy Forster in Mono County. At least he had seemed interested in the possible gang connection and sabotage angle. His phone rang seven times before going to voice mail. She left a message for him to call her. She made it sound as urgent as possible.

Frustrated, she called Ellen. The phone rang three times, then Ellen answered.

"Hi Maeva. I'm putting you on hold. I have the search people on the other line." Before Maeva could say anything the line went silent. At least something was happening. She waited patiently for Ellen to come on the line. It took only two minutes.

"Maeva, he's alive," Ellen said through guttural, racking sobs. Ellen was so stoic that Maeva had never seen or heard her cry or show weakness. She'd displayed fury a few times in Maeva's memory, but that's the only strong emotion she'd displayed. It was now obvious that Ellen had been holding in her dread. She could finally release the worst fear, at least temporarily.

"Where is he?"

It took a moment for Ellen to compose herself before replying. Maeva could hear another voice in the background. "My sister's here. Sorry, I …"

"It's okay,. That's great news. Where is he now? Is he okay?"

"No, I mean I don't know. The search team got to the plane and found one body laid out and burned. It was Crosby, the pilot."

"No sign of Cliff?"

"Yes, they were able to find a trail. He must have hiked out of the canyon. He's somewhere in the mountains. They've got a helicopter about to lift off now that they know there's a survivor."

"That's great news. I'm so happy for you." Maeva was surprised to see a drop of water land on her leg. Then she realized it came from her. She was crying, too. Her nose began to run. She snuffled it up and continued, "They'll find him. It'll be okay. Are you doing okay?"

"I will be. My sister's here."

Maeva's phone buzzed, indicating an incoming call. It was probably Forster calling her back. "I'm getting an incoming. I have to take it."

"I told them to call you next."

"Thank you. I'll talk to you soon." She punched the icon to switch to the incoming call. "Maeva Hanssen."

It was Forster. "Hi, returning your call. Your partner's alive. I just got off the phone with his wife."

"I know, I did, too. She put me on hold while she was talking to you."

"Good, so you know the status. We know he survived the crash and left. We still don't know where he is. He could be injured. We did find what looks like fresh blood on some rocks downstream."

This was new information that Ellen hadn't mentioned. Maybe Forster didn't want to give bad news to the wife but was willing to share with the partner. "A lot of blood?"

"No, a small smear. And they found some stones piled up where he climbed up to the top of the ridge. He was thinking smart. And if he could climb that canyon wall, he couldn't be too bad off. The big danger is dehydration or heatstroke."

"I heard they have a helicopter going up."

"Yes, it just took off. We have a possible area to search. It doesn't have any trails so it's not an easy ground search."

"What's the temperature there?"

"Nineties. There is water in the direction he's headed, if he can make it that far."

She was getting tired of the qualifiers and pessimistic "ifs" but it signified that he viewed her more as a fellow law enforcement colleague on a task than someone emotionally involved. Good. She could use that.

"Look, I called for another reason. I have some information. You know how I said to look for sabotage?"

"Yeah. I passed that on. The NTSB is there. Your information brought her there fast which wasn't an easy thing to make happen. I hope you're right."

Me too, thought Maeva. "Well I have a suspect who could have done it, and he's up there somewhere."

"A suspect? We don't even know there was any sabotage." The skepticism in his voice was palpable.

"Hear me out. It's a mechanic here at the airport where the plane took off. His name is Duc Bui. He goes by Doug."

"Doug? Yeah he's with the team. They told me he was an unprepared wimp. They didn't want him, but he tagged along until they let him join so he wouldn't get lost or injured on his own."

"Did he give a reason for being there?"

"I'm not sure. Something about contaminated gas or liability. Protecting the airport."

"Look, I know I'm going out on a limb and I don't want to ruin an innocent man's reputation, but he's not there representing the airport. I've spoken with the manager and they have no concerns about their gas being involved. He said Bui is the least qualified person he knows to go up in the mountains. But there is a reason he might be motivated."

"Look, it's bedlam here. I can't stay …"

"Listen! He might be there to kill Cliff. Cliff's the only remaining witness who can authenticate the key evidence – a recorded confession by a co-conspirator. If Cliff survives to testify and Bui is who I think he is, he's looking at life in prison."

"Whoa. An assassin with the search team? Don't you think that's a little far-fetched?"

"Yeah, it sounds pretty far out, I know."

"How would he know anyone survived?"

"I don't know. Maybe he wasn't there for that. Maybe he went to destroy any evidence of sabotage before the NTSB found it. Or maybe he just wanted to make sure they were both dead. I've confirmed that he knows the sister of one of the murderers."

"I don't know either, Maeva, but I tell you what I'll do. I'll tell the leader to keep an eye on him and not let him touch the plane or debris and not leave the group."

"Good. That's a good idea. Thank you."

That was as much as she could hope for at this point, so she ended the call. Then she called Melissa Ingram to update her on the fact that Bui was now with the search team. Melissa told her that she hadn't heard any more from the gang task force detective, but assured her they were looking into him.

Chapter 15

"It's been over an hour," Randy announced. "He hasn't replied to any of our voices. We haven't found his body and there are no vultures circling. He's not here. Come on, Trish, we have to go back. You heard Darryl."

"Just a little farther. There's some foliage up ahead. This is the first real greenery we've come to. That would be where I'd stop if I were stranded out here. If we don't find anything, we turn around."

"That's what you said at the last spot. I'm serious, we need to go back. It'll take us until four at least."

"We're almost there. I swear, this is the last spot." She didn't wait for him to reply, or, worse, grab her and force her back the other way. He couldn't leave her alone out here. He had to follow her. It didn't take long. Trish spotted the first trench Cliff had dug. She reached down and touched the bottom. It was damp to the touch. "Over here."

"Well, I'll be damned. He must have been desperate for water. But you can't get anything potable that way. It'll all dry up as soon as it seeps in. It's over ninety."

"It's damp. This is midday. Once the sun goes behind the mountain the shade will protect it. Maybe he waited until evening when it started to cool. There could be some accumulation in the bottom."

"How could he get it out? A straw?" Randy snorted sarcastically.

"I don't know. You could get a small tube in there."

"A tube? You think he wore lipstick?" He laughed at his own joke.

"Don't be an ass. Maybe he had chapstick or sunscreen or something that would fit. Maybe he soaked a sock in it and sucked it out after. People can be resourceful when their life depends on it."

"We have to go back."

"What!? Now we know we're on the right track. Darryl said to go back if we didn't find anything. We found something."

"He said to come back if we didn't find *him*. That's a person, not a hole in the ground."

"Well, tell him what we found and ask him. For all we know he's a few hundred yards ahead."

"He had a three-day head start. The only way he's that close is if he died."

"At least radio Darryl. He needs to know. This will help the helicopter search."

Randy had to accept that advice. The whole search team had to know of this find. He tried to raise Darryl on the radio, but once again the reception sucked. He'd have to go back up on the ridge top again. They had to stay together for safety, so Trish agreed to follow him back up the canyon wall. Even she was getting tired now and it would be an exhausting return to the plane site. First, though, she pulled some pink marking tape from her pack and tied a big bow on the top of the bush closest to the trench. Then the two of them set off for higher ground.

When he reached the ridgeline, Randy tried the radio again.

"Randy to Darryl."

"Darryl. Go ahead."

"We found something. He dug a hole in a bushy area. He was obviously digging for water."

"Are you headed back?"

"We could go on, but we're not well-equipped for an overnight stay here."

"You were supposed to turn around after an hour."

Randy shot Trish an I-told-you-so look. "Sorry. We're ready to head back."

"What's your location?"

"We headed north from the crash site and then east over the ridge after about a mile. From there we headed down whatever stream this is. I don't know if it has a name. It's a dry creekbed, probably feeds into White Creek. We're maybe four miles hiking distance from you."

"It's too late for that. Give me your exact coordinates. I'll have to send the copter for you. Is there a place for it to land?"

"No, but we're on the ridge. It's clear above us. It's an easy spot to drop a line." Randy turned on his phone and tapped the hiking app he used. He waited for it to lock into the GPS satellites. When it did, he read the coordinates to Darryl.

"Okay, Got it. Stay there. We've had a development. They found evidence the plane was sabotaged."

"Seriously? So how does that change things?"

"Is Doug with you guys?"

Trish gave Randy a look like Darryl had just asked if they'd grown purple wings. "Doug? The airport guy? No. He went back."

"Apparently he didn't. I don't have cell coverage here, but I had Forster call him. Doug should have been back an hour ago, certainly in phone range. His phone isn't on the system."

"Maybe he forgot to turn it back on, or the battery died."

"There's more to it than that. Forster'll explain when you get back. Just be on the lookout for him. He could be somewhere on the mountain. Look, I'm staying overnight here with the NTSB woman to preserve the crime scene. The copter dropped off a tent, some food, and other supplies and picked up the others. They're being shuttled back to where we left the van. They'll come back for you."

"I thought it was supposed to be searching for the survivor."

"Change of plan. We'll talk later. Just sit tight."

"Roger. Out."

Randy and Trish settled in for the wait. They'd been on search teams together once or twice in the past, but had never been teamed up as a pair. They didn't know each other well. Randy found out that Trish was an avid skier. She'd almost made the U.S. Olympic team ten years earlier, but just wasn't good enough. Until a week ago she worked as a camp counselor at one of the local summer camps for rich kids, although the camp had closed for the school year. During the winter she taught skiing in Tahoe. She was divorced with no kids but didn't seem bitter about it.

Trish already assumed Randy was adopted and didn't ask about his birth parentage. She didn't refrain out of political correctness; she just thought it would be impolite. It didn't matter to her what his ethnic background was. She was interested to learn he was a former marine and enjoyed crocheting. In his gear it was hard to see, but she could tell he had a good body. He was also single and cute. She was aching to ask him if he had a girlfriend but wasn't brave enough. She was three years older and three inches taller than he was. He knew she was divorced, so single. It would have to be up to him to make the first move.

Chapter 16

The first shot hit Cliff in the thigh just above the knee. He felt the impact, but not the pain. Not at first. Bui's second shot went wide, which is common with automatic weapons. The first shot's recoil moves the barrel and the shooter doesn't have enough time to correct it for number two. At one thousand rounds a minute in full auto mode, the second shot is almost instantaneous.

Cliff rolled to the side and came up into a crouch, gun in hand. Bui was charging at him, holding the Glock like it was a club. Cliff pointed his gun, Crosby's Sig Sauer, at the center of mass and pulled the trigger three times. Bui crumpled onto his knees and then curled over and fell onto his side in a fetal position.

The first shot had pierced the liver, the next one the lungs, and the third one had shattered his left humerus. Bui was moaning softly and clutching his midsection. Cliff may not have been a very good shot, but his FBI training had served him well. Handguns are intended for close combat, not distance firing. Bui had been five to eight feet away when the rounds hit. You don't aim at that distance. You point at the center of mass. It doesn't matter if the target is blurry. It's all about timing and muscle memory from the training. There's a common standard bandied about saying "three yards, three shots, three seconds" to describe a typical gunfight. It may or may not be based on scientific study, but it was pretty close in this case.

Cliff tried to stand, but his leg wouldn't let him. Bui's gun was still there within the man's reach. Cliff lunged, pushing off with his good knee and one hand and grabbed the Glock's barrel. He yanked the gun away as he cursed. The barrel had burned the palm of his hand. At least it was safely out of the attacker's reach. Cliff looked at the Glock and saw why there had only been two shots. An empty shell casing was jammed in the chamber, preventing another round from loading. That's another drawback of automatic and even semi-automatic weapons. Sometimes the shell being ejected doesn't clear the chamber in time for the next round. This is especially true if the gun is not well-cleaned and even more so if it's been modified for automatic fire. Bui's lack of gun care had made the difference between life and death.

Cliff dragged himself next to Bui, who lay moaning, gasping, and spewing red foam from the hole in his chest. He wasn't dead yet, but his chances didn't look good. Cliff wanted as much information from him as possible.

"Are there others coming for me?" Cliff demanded.

"Kill me, please. I can't take it," Bui gasped.

"Answer me. Are you alone?"

"Others. Team coming… please. I'm dying. Quick … " he screamed as a tsunami of pain swept over him.

Cliff felt through the man's pockets and found his cell phone. The phone was on, but the screen was locked. He noticed the oval on the back. It had a fingerprint ID feature like Cliff's own phone. He grabbed the man's right hand and pressed his forefinger against the opening. The screen came to life. Cliff touched the camera button and then the record icon for video. The red light confirmed he was recording with audio.

"Tell me who killed Raven Tran."

Bui collected himself and choked out, "If I tell, will you do it?"

"Sure. I'll end your suffering. Spill."

"Dice. Spiked her dose with fentanyl."

"That was in San Jose?"

"Yeah. Do it now. Please …"

That was the last word Bui spoke. Cliff would never have killed Bui, despite the promise. It wasn't out of compassion for this criminal, but out of respect for the law. Cliff was a big supporter of euthanasia, but it was still against the law. That, plus the guy deserved to suffer and wasn't going to last long anyway. He wasn't about to risk a murder charge. With one hand he shook the man several times, keeping the video going with the other. Then he slapped Bui's face while calling to him to wake up. When he opened the man's eyes and the pupils didn't dilate, he announced that the man was dead and stopped the video.

Now what?

Cliff considered his options. The man's phone was still working. Cliff tried to call 911, but got a message that there was no signal. The battery was also low. He went to the email icon and tapped it. It showed the last email, no doubt stored in a cache. The email was meaningless commercial business about some online training course.

He went back to the video and tapped the share icon, then tapped the option to share to email. He typed in his own email address and then CC'ed Ellen's, then tapped the send icon. The phone responded that it was unable to send due to no signal. That was all he could think of to do with the phone. He hoped that when the phone got to cell reception it would automatically send the queued video. He was about to turn it off to preserve the battery when he noticed that there was a phone finder app still open. He tapped it to show full screen. An icon at the top showed that it had no signal, but the main screen was a map with a red dot and a set of coordinates. The map didn't have enough detail to be certain, but Cliff recognized that the coordinates had to be close to the present location, within a few miles anyway.

Next he examined his own leg wound. It was a clean through-and-through. There was minimal bleeding and it hadn't shattered the bone, but the muscle was badly torn up. There was no way he could hike on that leg, not for the distances he needed. He ripped a strip off Bui's shirt. The bullet holes helped to make that easy. He used that to bind the bullet wound.

The next order of business was his safety. The man, whose name Cliff still didn't know, had said there was a team. A team sent to kill him? Or to rescue him? Was he lying? There was no way to know. He'd seemed desperate for that final mercy shot. Cliff ejected the magazine of his own gun. There were only three rounds left. He'd tossed the other magazine a ways back to reduce weight. Having ammunition now seemed like a higher priority than it had been.

He removed the magazine from the Glock. Fortunately, it took the same caliber rounds as Crosby's, standard 9mm. Cliff didn't trust the Glock, since it had jammed, so he extracted rounds from that magazine until he had enough to fill his own gun's magazine. Jim would have kept his gun clean. Then he reinserted the magazine in the Sig Sauer. He felt better being fully loaded in case there was an attack. And the weight shouldn't matter, since he wasn't going anywhere anytime soon.

Once that was over, he felt like he could take a breath and think more long term. He pulled Bui's backpack off, which was no easy task with Cliff's limited mobility and Bui's no mobility. He was, quite literally, dead weight. Inside Cliff found one full bottle of water and two empty ones. There was also a candy bar. Cliff took that and ripped it open immediately. He took one bite of the candy bar and reveled in its richness. He followed that with a swig of water. He wanted more of both, but was afraid of the consequences if he ate too much after being starved. He stored both of these for later.

There was a second clip of ammo in the backpack and a sweatshirt along with a pack of latex gloves. What had he wanted the gloves for? A set of tools completed the contents – two wrenches, a screwdriver, something that looked like tin snips, a clamp, and a piercing tool like an awl. The tools were an even bigger mystery. If he was sent to kill Cliff, why was this man carrying them? They added useless weight.

Suddenly, it hit him. How had this man found him out here? How had he even known he was alive? It had to have been the emergency phone in the first aid kit. It hadn't been put there by Jim; it had been planted to track the plane. That's why the phone finder app was open on the gunman's phone. That would explain why the first aid kit phone had a charge on it when Cliff had found it. This man must have charged it fully and stashed it in the kit before the plane took off and expected it would lead him to the crash site when it went down. He must have sabotaged the plane and was going to remove evidence of the sabotage. That's why he needed the tools and gloves.

That left open the question of who else could track him? Surely the dead guy, as Cliff thought of him, wouldn't have shared the app or password with any rescuers. He might have done so with others in his gang. If so, they would have come together and converged on him, at least that's the way it worked in the FBI when making an arrest. Since that hadn't happened, he was probably operating alone. So what did that comment about a team mean?

The one thing Cliff knew was that he was not going to get out on his own. He had to be found. He would just have to take his chances on who it was. He had to hope the reference about a team was to rescuers and hope that they were in the area. He counted out in his head the rounds fired during the gunfight. It was hard to remember. There were three holes in dead guy and one leg wound for him, so it was at least four shots. If anyone had been in the vicinity, they would have heard them. But handgun shots weren't as loud as rifle shots. The bullets didn't travel at supersonic speeds. Blocked by the trees, the sound wouldn't carry more than a half mile, he guessed. There was no point in shooting any more right now. He'd have to wait until he had reason to believe someone was in earshot. He had limited ammunition.

He went back to searching the body and went into the pockets. Dead guy had a wallet. Inside was a Nevada driver's license and some credit cards as well as $180 in cash. Business cards identified him as Doug Bui, airline avionics specialist. The driver's license showed the name as Duc Bui. Doug and Duc. Interesting. Could this be the unknown "Duck?"

He was tempted to explore Bui's phone more, but he was afraid of running the battery down to nothing. He didn't see how it could help him get rescued while he was still out of cell phone range. He used one trick to guarantee he could get access later, then shut it off. At least if he didn't make it, the phone might eventually be found, and when turned on would send that video of Bui's blaming Dice for Raven's death. That was a federal crime, traveling across state lines to commit murder. If Dice beat the state charge, he might get convicted for that one.

For now, there wasn't much he could do but wait. It was getting dark and he'd have to overnight here with the body. The thought made him queasy. He scooted away a few yards and grabbed his bindle from the rock. He wrapped himself in the space blanket and made himself as comfortable as he could a few yards farther from the body.

The helicopter hovered overhead and lowered the harness. Trish took the first ride up and sent it back down for Randy. There was no observer since the pilot didn't want the extra weight. He was on a pickup run. Once Trish and Randy were aboard, they could serve as observers. The plan was to overfly the search area for the next half hour while there was light and then drop the two back at the ski area where the vehicles had parked.

Trish directed the pilot to follow the canyon out to where it bifurcated into a north passage and east passage. She and Randy scanned the landscape as the craft slowly followed her directions. The terrain was steep granite canyon walls with patches of scrub foliage, mostly rock cress, dwarf bilberry, and shieldleaf. Lower down near Mono Lake in the pumice flats the lupine grew abundantly and spread a startling violet blanket over the land when in bloom. Sagebrush dominated the drier, flatter open areas. In clusters near the creekbed groves of trees thrived. These included several varieties of pines, and even willow in the wettest areas. Trish knew these plants well because she had been taking kids on nature hikes all summer. She'd had to learn them. She was hoping someday to come upon Methuselah, a bristlecone pine believed to be the oldest living thing on the planet at almost 5000 years.

Its exact location is a well-kept secret to prevent vandalism or injury from careless eco-tourists. Some thoughtless geocacher might hang a doodad on it and others would break it apart climbing on it. It was across the highway in the White Range, that much she knew.

She set aside these thoughts. They were not on a horticultural mission. They were looking for a lone individual in need of help. They didn't know anything about him beyond the fact he was a male in his 50s or 60s. They didn't know what equipment he might have with him or what clothing. They had been able to infer certain things about him from their search. He had managed to find water and was staying near the creek. He'd made a cairn to guide rescuers. He was apparently resourceful and not seriously injured, although there had been that one smear of blood. All they could do was follow their instincts and concentrate on the areas where they would have most likely have gone had they been in the same position.

Randy sat on the opposite side of the copter from Trish and dutifully scanned the terrain, but his mind sometimes drifted. In particular, it drifted toward the woman sitting next to him. He already had an on again-off again girlfriend, but right now they were off again. Trish wasn't a beauty, but she wasn't bad looking. She had the sleek muscular body of a thoroughbred and he was impressed with her fitness and endurance.

At first he had taken umbrage at her assertiveness. Randy considered himself the leader of this two-man search party. Darryl had told him to "take Trish downstream." To him, that meant putting him in charge. Trish hadn't seen it that way. She'd called him an ass. Well, not really. She'd said not to be an ass, but it amounted to the same thing. She'd insisted they continue searching and then they'd found the trench the survivor had dug. She'd been right. Her instincts were as good as or better than his. He respected that now even if it had bugged him at the time. He should have made more of an effort to make mutual decisions.

He thought about asking her for her number, but the thought made him nervous. What if she refused? It would be awkward and make it hard to work together on the search. Maybe he should wait until the search was over. Besides, she was taller than he was. Tall girls don't go out with short guys, a fact he'd learned the hard way. Nah. She'd turn him down for sure. He forced himself to refocus on the search.

The allotted time passed without any sign of the survivor. The pilot took them back to the ski area lot. Forster was there waiting for them along with the team members who weren't staying at the crash site.

"Good work on finding that waterhole," Forster said as they entered. There was no shaking of hands or pats on the back. There was a life at stake, so it was all down to brass tacks. "Did you mark the coordinates of the hole? The ones I have are on top of the ridge where they picked you up."

"I have them," Trish said. "The hole is just down the hillside from the ones you have. It won't be hard to find again."

The deputy noted that the phrasing indicated Trish was expecting to go on searching there. That was fine with him, as he had intended to send these two back the next day. "Good. It's getting too dark to keep searching today. Tomorrow you two go with Darryl and try to follow the tracks.

"How are we going to get there?" Randy asked.

"We need to take advantage of all the sunlight we have. The chopper will take you to the crash site where we'll pick Darryl up in the harness, then it'll take the three of you to the point where we just picked you up. You can continue the search from there."

"The canyon's too deep for the chopper at the crash site. You can't get the harness cable down far enough from above and the opening is too narrow for the chopper to go down between the walls."

"Darryl knows that. He'll be on the ridge. We're also going to give you guys a satellite phone. The radio isn't working well down in the canyons and ravines."

"So what do we do now?" Trish asked.

"Give me a complete debrief of what you saw today. Then I'll have a patrol car drop you back at the motel. Get to bed early. Someone will pick you up at 6:15 tomorrow. Be ready."

Randy and Trish glanced at each other and nodded. Randy proceeded to give Forster a rundown of everything he could remember about the search and the crash site. Trish corrected a few details and added a few more.

Chapter 17

Cliff woke up the next morning shortly after daybreak. He wasn't sure how he'd managed to sleep, but somehow he had. The tissue around his bullet wound hurt badly. He realized he hadn't dressed it properly. The first aid kit had some kind of antiseptic cream. He was able to reach his bindle from where he lay, so he hauled it over to him and pulled out the kit.

He didn't want to take off his jeans. Not only would that hurt, especially where the fabric was stuck to his skin with blood, but he wasn't sure he'd be able to get them back on with the swelling. So he squirted the cream on his finger and rubbed it on his skin through the open bullet hole. It hurt, but he clenched his teeth and put up with the pain.

He maneuvered himself into a semi-standing position, with his weight on his uninjured leg and leaning against the large rock on which his bindle rested. He pointed himself away from his makeshift campsite and released a stream of urine. It was the most urine he'd been able to produce in over twenty-four hours.

With effort, he managed to move using one leg and both hands like a three-legged alien from some Grade B sci-fi movie. He made it to the nearby stream to fill his water bottle. He drank the entire bottle in one session, stopping for only a few seconds halfway through. Then he filled the bottle again. He'd brought one of Bui's bottles, too, and filled that. He returned with his crabwalk to his bindle.

He remembered the candy bar. He found that and ate the rest of it. He silently berated himself for not rationing it, but his hunger pangs gave him no choice.

Out of nowhere, a loud noise penetrated the air. Suddenly, a helicopter was flying overhead. He looked up but couldn't see it through the tree cover against the bright sky. Just as quickly it passed out of hearing. It had been close; even though he hadn't seen it, the noise made that clear. They must be searching for him. He grabbed the gun and fired it once into a nearby tree. He didn't want to hit the copter accidentally. He waited ten minutes to see if there was any response, but there was none. He put the gun down.

Stupid!, he thought. He'd ridden in a helicopter. The noise inside is deafening. Everyone wears ear protection. The gunshot may seem earsplitting at ground level, but there was no way they'd hear it inside the helicopter even directly overhead. He'd wasted a bullet.

Still, this was a good sign. Whatever gang Bui had belonged to, he was sure they didn't have a helicopter. That meant it was a legitimate search and rescue group doing the looking. He just needed to get their attention. From the speed of the helicopter, he was pretty sure they weren't doing a search for him. Aircraft move slowly when looking for signs of life below. Maybe they'd found the crash site and were sending in a team of investigators there. It could very well have been transporting people or equipment to that site.

This, too, could be a positive sign. Even if they were only going to the crash site, that meant they'd located it and must know that one person was alive. If they weren't searching for him right this minute, they soon would be. But that didn't mean Bui's gang didn't have anyone else looking for him. He kept the gun in hand. Whether for defense or to signal rescuers, he felt more secure armed.

Chapter 18

Ellen's sister Theresa didn't have to look up the number. She needed only to tap the icon in her contacts. The retired director of the FBI was the godfather of her child and a close family friend. He'd been even more than that when her husband Mark had died. He was something of a protector, a guardian, for her whole family. Mark had been his best friend when they'd both been attorneys at the Department of Justice. She tapped the icon.

"Theresa, how are you? How's Ashley?"

"Hi, Larry. I'm okay, Ashley, too, but Ellen isn't."

"What's going on?"

"Have you heard about Cliff?"

"Ellen's husband? No."

"He's missing. He was on a light plane that crashed in the Sierras."

"That was him? I heard something on the news, but there were no names. That's terrible. Is there a chance he's survived?"

"Yes, he has survived. That much we know. It's probably not out on the news yet. A team was sent expecting just a recovery operation, but when they got to the crash site, they found only the pilot's body. Cliff was the passenger. They found a trail. He's alive."

"Is there something I can do to help?"

"I'm not sure. He was there on Bureau business. Flying, I mean. They'd both been subpoenaed to appear in a case in Las Vegas, something related to when they were in the Bureau. Maeva thinks it's gang-related and that he may be hunted by the gang. He's like the last witness or something."

"Who's Maeva?"

"Cliff's partner at the PI firm. A cute redhead. You've probably seen her standing modestly behind him during some of those press conferences or award ceremonies. She's a real pistol and a good investigator. Ellen respects her abilities."

"Cute redhead, huh. If I said I remembered her that might be self-incriminating. So has the FBI become involved?"

"No. Ellen is too distraught and too by-the-book to try to pull strings, but I don't give a crap. If you can do anything through your FBI contacts, I'm asking you to do it."

"It doesn't matter if he's retired. It's still an FBI duty he's carrying out. If he's being threatened or hunted, that's a direct assault on the FBI as a whole. If I was still there, I'd spare no resources to find him. Did you call the main FBI number?"

"I thought it would be faster going through you. I'm sorry if …"

"Don't be sorry. It was smart. Give me all the contact information you have and I'll take care of it."

Theresa filled him in and ended the call. Then she went into the kitchen where Ellen was sitting at the island with a cup of tea. That was the only room that still had a land line. Cliff and Ellen mostly used their cells, but the land line was still the most reliable number technically, and too many contacts and companies still had that as their number, so they'd kept it all these years.

"I just called Larry," Theresa declared with a touch of defiance.

"The ex-Director? Tee, you shouldn't have done that. I've been accused of being the Director's pet before. I could get in trouble."

"Shush. You didn't do anything. I did. Besides, he said that it was FBI business even if Cliff's retired. He said he was going to take care of it."

"How? What could he do?"

"I don't know. He's got the whole FBI behind him. He must be able to do something."

Ellen nodded and leaned over to give Theresa a hug. "Thanks, sis." The familiar sound of children squabbling resounded from the living room. Ellen called out "Tommy, Mia, knock it off. We're trying to talk in here." The volume of the squabbling only increased. Ellen looked torn between sticking by Theresa and handling the kids.

Theresa put a hand on Ellen's arm. "You go. It sounds like they need a mother, not the fun auntie. I'm right here by the phone. I gave Larry this number."

Ellen thanked her again and launched into mediator/disciplinarian mode and she headed for the living room. Thirty minutes later the kitchen phone rang. Ellen was in the process of changing Mia's diaper since she was still not fully potty trained, so Theresa answered it.

"It's for you," she yelled into the hallway.

"Coming." Ellen hurried out to the kitchen still drying her hands. "Hello, this is Ellen."

"Ellen, this is Maria Alvarado. I hear your husband is in trouble."

"Director Alvarado, uh, I didn't expect … I mean I didn't ask for…"

"I know that. Larry called and filled me in, but I want to get the whole story from you. Someone in my office will look up the old unlawful flight case, but that won't help much right now. Larry didn't know the subject's name."

"Cliff, well, he's a former agent and so was the other man, Jim Crosby, the pilot. They're both retired now. When they were agents they arrested a woman on the UFAP-murder warrant and she voluntarily confessed. She made a tape. I don't know all the details, but it implicated two other men. I don't even know the names. I didn't pay much attention at the time. Cliff isn't active in that sort of thing now. He runs a private investigation firm now."

"I know who he is. He's been something of a thorn in the side of the FBI in the past, but he's part of the FBI family."

"Well, he only did what …"

"Okay, stop. I'm sorry I phrased it that way. It's just that he has a certain reputation. He's a very good investigator, I know, and he got good results. His methods were sometimes just … unconventional. My apologies. Like I said, he's part of the FBI family. If he was working an FBI case, even compelled by subpoena after retirement, he deserves the same support I'd give an active duty agent. Can you tell me how to identify the case and who's in charge of the search?"

"It's a local murder case out of Las Vegas. The D.A.'s office there will know. The subject had a Vietnamese name. The contact for the search is a Deputy Forster with the Mono County Sheriff's office. That's a California County on the Nevada state line." She gave Alvarado the contact number.

"That's good. We have resources they don't have. I've already notified the SAC in Sacramento to get a team to deploy. They have our best heat-sensing technology in the western part of the country. It will take some time to get them there, I'm afraid. I'll also notify the local office … who is that, do you know?"

"I'm not sure who covers Mono County. I think Sacramento has a resident agency in South Lake Tahoe and one in Fresno. Reno R.A. might be able to help, too. They're under Las Vegas."

"Shame on me. You know the field offices better than I do."

"No, I don't. We work with Sacramento Division all the time, that's all. You have the whole country to learn and you've only been Director for a year. I've been in almost twenty years. I don't know a thing about ninety percent of the offices."

"You're being generous. Anyway, I need to know more about this threat. Larry said something about him being hunted."

"Well, that's a theory. Cliff's partner, Maeva Hanssen, is in Las Vegas now. She's been doing some investigating and talking to the A.D.A. prosecuting the murder case. She knows more about that than I do. She found out that the defense subpoenaed Cliff and Jim and paid Cliff extra travel fees if he rode in a private plane, Jim's plane."

"The defense subpoenaed them? That's not normal."

"No. So then at the hearing the defense waived the right to cross them even though they'd subpoenaed them. All they had to do was authenticate the confession tape of the woman, but they never got the chance. So now Jim's dead and Cliff is the only one who can authenticate it at trial. Then some Vietnamese mechanic from the airport in Vegas has gone off joining the search party. Maeva suspects he sabotaged the plane and wanted to either destroy evidence of that or to kill any survivor."

"Maeva. Is she a former agent, too?"

"No, she's young. She dropped out of Stanford Law. She's a good investigator and devoted to Cliff. I'd trust her with my life."

"Give me her contact info."

Ellen did.

"Anyway, I have to go. I'll get in touch with some people to coordinate our response. I'll be following this, but I'm going to turn over operations to them. I don't know the resources or the geography like they do."

Something hit him on the shoulder. Cliff jerked violently in reaction and cranked off a round involuntarily. The gun was still in his hand. It took him a moment to realize what had happened: a pine cone had fallen on him. He looked up. All the pines around him were laden with bunches of them, like clusters of hand grenades ready to be deployed. The ground was littered with them, too. And he'd fired the gun without meaning to. He was too jumpy. He needed to calm down. He put the gun away.

Cliff recognized the smell with alarm. Smoke! Flashes of memory of the plane crash assaulted him. He shook those off and looked around to try to locate the source. It was only a few feet away, behind him to his right. A wisp of smoke was rising from the pine needles and twigs.

He crabwalked over to the spot and realized what had happened. The shell casing from that last shot he'd taken had landed in the dry pine needles, twigs, and leaves. It had begun smoldering, but so far there was no blaze. He immediately poured water on it from his bottle until it sizzled out. He dug around with his foot to make sure it was all out. If a wildfire started here, he'd have no chance of escaping it with his limited mobility.

Still, this gave him an idea. There must be some sort of fire watch going on in these mountains. CalFire has been super vigilant since the mega fires have begun plaguing the state over the last few years. If he could start a controlled fire, just enough to send a plume of smoke aloft, that could bring rescue. The risk, of course, was that it could get out of control and kill him, perhaps even kill others and destroy homes.

He gathered a handful of pine needles, twigs, and cones and made his way back to the stream. He surveyed the area. Downstream a few yards was a large rock, a boulder really, with a relatively flat top. If he could start the fire there and keep watch to be sure sparks and embers didn't ignite anything else, he felt he could do it. But how could he start the fire?

One thing he didn't have was a match. If he'd had his glasses he might be able to focus a sunbeam, but the one good lens he'd had had been dropped during the shootout and was essentially invisible to him now among the detritus on the ground. His vision without the glasses wasn't good enough to read his GPS unit or anything else. There was no way he'd find it.

He could shoot the gun again, hoping to start a fire, but that entailed yet more risks. Shooting into the trees could start a fire in unwanted spots, either where the bullet hit a tree, or wherever the shell landed. Both are very hot after firing. The bullet could ricochet and hit him. If he shot into the air over the trees, the bullet could still be hot enough to start a fire wherever it landed. He couldn't shoot directly into a pile of tinder on the rock as the bullet would definitely ricochet. On top of all this, he could use up his ammunition shooting multiple times and still not succeed in starting a fire. The shots from the earlier gunfight hadn't.

He contemplated this while he refilled his bottle. He'd emptied one of them putting out the smoldering area. At least here he had water, but he was very hungry again. The effort he'd made moving back and forth from his bindle to the stream had exhausted him. His leg wound throbbed with pain, too. He was going to have to decide on a spot and gather his stuff there where he wouldn't have to move.

Darryl put down the satellite phone. "Okay, here's the plan. We'll start where you two found the hole and work our way downstream. We'll keep calling out to him. His name is Cliff. There's another team starting at the meadow by Obsidian Dome. The chopper can land there. It's just a guess, but that's where you thought was the most likely point he'd reach if he continued. They'll work their way up Glass creek towards us, also calling out to him."

"Who's on the other team?" Trish asked.

"Forster's going to lead it with one other deputy. The FBI has sent two agents, too. They're waiting for the copter to shuttle them in. We got the first ride. It's not back there yet. It can only carry four including the pilot, so only one of those agents can ride with them. The other one's an aviation specialist. He'll be dropped at the crash site later to help the NTSB woman. The FBI's flying in a plane from Fresno with thermal imaging gear. That should arrive late afternoon. It won't be deployed until the evening. Thermal imaging works best at night when the ground has cooled off."

"Will the agents be armed?" Randy asked.

"I assume so. They're now working on the assumption that the plane was sabotaged to keep the two retired guys from testifying in a murder case. They suspect Doug of being on the hunt for him. If we spot him, don't say anything to let him know we're onto him – I mean, that he's a suspect. Don't confront him or anything. He may be armed."

"Doug? Our Doug? The tagalong guy?"

"Yeah."

"So Doug's whereabouts are unknown?"

"Right."

Trish's expression showed she wasn't satisfied. "What about a visual air search?"

"Once everybody has been shuttled around, the helicopter will be cruising the whole area."

"Okay," Trish said. "So let's get going. There's a man out here injured and in need of food." She began down the makeshift trail from the ridge top to the creekbed below.

Darryl and Randy followed right behind. Ten minutes later they were at the bush where Trish had tied the bow. She showed Randy the trench Cliff had dug. There was a pool of water at the bottom that had accumulated overnight. Darryl nodded approvingly. This victim had found water where there wasn't any visible. He could still be alive.

The three of them spread out around the site looking for any other clues as to Cliff's condition or his thinking. Darryl found a footprint in one of the softer spots of earth, but he couldn't tell if it was from Cliff or from the search Randy and Trish had done the previous day. After fifteen minutes they decided that this site held no more useful information, so they headed downstream. They took turns hollering Cliff's name every minute or two.

Dice cursed his phone and turned it off. Duck was still not answering. It showed an out of service message. He was probably still in the mountains outside cell phone range. Dice had tried the phone finder app since he had that set up for Duck's phone. It showed him unmoving at a spot off the June Lake Loop near the plane crash, but that was as of the previous day. That's probably where he'd left cell phone range. The app couldn't locate him until he turned it back on in range of a tower. He should have returned to the motel overnight, or if he'd been successful taking out the target, been home by now. He had to assume Duck was out there still searching for the surviving agent. He heard a guard approaching and hid the phone.

"Visitor for you, Truong," the guard announced.

He wasn't expecting any visitor. "Who is it?"

"A woman. Good-looking."

This piqued his curiosity. His lawyer had a good-looking associate, if you liked the 40-ish type, but he didn't know her to visit the jail. Maybe she was carrying a message. He stood and nodded. The guard handcuffed him as he exited the cell.

Once out in the visitor area he looked around. He didn't see the secretary. He looked at the guard who pointed out a redhead sitting alone at a table in the far corner. He didn't know her, but he remembered Duck saying something about a woman nosing around the airport. This must be her. The guard walked him over to that table and recuffed him through a metal bar affixed to the table, then left to stand in the corner. Truong wasn't about to say anything to her, but he was curious, so he sat opposite to her.

"Hello, Dice," Maeva said.

"Who are you?"

"My name's Maeva. I'm Cliff Knowles's partner."

Truong didn't respond.

"Cliff Knowles. You know, one of the agents you tried to kill with the sabotaged plane."

"You can't talk to me without my lawyer present. I know my rights."

"Apparently you don't. I can talk to you. I'm not a cop. I'm just the woman who's going to kill you if Cliff doesn't survive."

Truong snorted derisively. "I'm quaking in my boots."

"I don't care about your case. Anything you tell me will be excluded anyway. I just want him back safe. Tell me how to find him."

"You're cute when you're angry."

"The Mr. Cool Dude act doesn't get you anywhere. Where's Doug?"

Truong's eyes widened for a moment. He tried to hide his surprise. He'd never been tied to Duc Bui by the police. He wasn't sure if she had made the connection. The audio recording Raven had made talked about Duck, but the cops didn't know who that was. Even Raven hadn't known who he was. This woman might just be bluffing, throwing out the name she'd heard wrong. He didn't respond.

"He's not at the airport," she went on. "Is he out trying to finish off the last witness?"

That answered that. She had made the connection. She knew who Duck was. That wasn't good. When he got back, Duck would be pulled in for questioning. Duck was probably the smartest member of the gang, after himself, of course, but Truong wasn't sure how tough he'd be under questioning. He'd never been through the justice system the way most of the street punks had. He remained silent.

"The FBI is on the case now. You sent him across state lines to kill Cliff. That makes it a federal case. Even if you beat the state charge, you're facing a long stretch. If Cliff dies, it's life without parole. There's no parole in the federal system. You're better off cooperating. Tell us how to find Duck and Cliff. You can make a deal with the D.A. on your current case and be out in ten or fifteen."

"So your partner, he's not dead?"

"They're saying the pilot died, but Cliff survived. The search is on now and the FBI just joined that. He'll be found sooner or later. It'll be better for you if he's alive when they do. Tell me how to find Duck. At least we can pull him off the hunt. If Cliff dies of exposure or injuries from the crash, it'll be hard to prove sabotage caused it. But if Duck kills him, then you're both looking at life. Since Cliff's an FBI agent, you'll get solitary confinement. Make it easy on yourself. Tell me how you communicate with Duck. Is your lawyer conveying the orders?"

"That's enough. I don't have to listen to this crap." Truong yelled to the guard that the interview, or whatever this was, was over.

The guard returned, unlocked the cuffs to relock them after unhooking them from the metal pole, and led him back to the cell area. Maeva sat, frustrated, for a minute but another guard called her name and told her she had to leave now that the prisoner had returned to his cell. She got up and left.

Outside she considered her options. She hadn't gotten any useful information. She'd picked up on his expression when she'd mentioned Duck. Apparently he'd thought no one knew about Bui. Maybe that would give him some anxious nights. He'd asked her if Cliff was alive. She didn't know how much he heard from the outside world, but he might not have known for sure Cliff was still alive, or at least believed to be alive.

She could call Ingram and share this, but she saw no point. That would just give the defense another arrow in its quiver. If she called Ingram and briefed her, it could potentially be interpreted as her having been sent to question Truong without his lawyer being present. In truth, Ingram knew nothing about the interview. It had been Maeva's idea.

She had concluded that Truong must be communicating with Bui by phone. If she could get his phone number, it might be trackable. It was probably a burner phone, but it might still be possible. If it could be geolocated, the sheriff or FBI might be able to get to Bui before he got to Cliff.

This hadn't worked out as she'd hoped. She regretted her comment about being the woman who'd kill him. She'd been pissed at his attitude and had let her anger overcome her judgment. The conversations in the visiting area were almost certainly recorded. She may even have committed a crime, although she didn't think a hypothetical threat like she'd made was prosecutable. She'd just have to try something else, but she was fresh out of ideas.

Chapter 19

The pile of tinder was in place on the rock. The needles had been blowing off in the moderate breeze, so he'd built a sort of shelter out of cones and sticks and filled it in with needles almost like a bird's nest. Cliff had both water bottles full, just in case.

He took a spot downstream of the rock so he could fire upstream into a small muddy area where the water trickled down. That minimized the chance of ricochet and starting a fire. He knew the shell casing ejected to the right, too, so positioned this way, the shell would land in or near the stream. He couldn't see well enough to really aim, but he wasn't trying to hit an exact spot. His thought was to hold the gun parallel to the ground just over the tinder pile so that the flames from the gunpowder's combustion gases would ignite the needles. It wasn't obvious during daytime, but he'd been in night shoots during training and knew that flames shot from the barrel of a handgun when fired.

He decided everything was lined up and ready. He pulled the trigger. The blast of hot gases tore through the pile sending pine cones rolling off the rock. Dry needles flew through the air in flames, landing mostly in the stream or on its banks. Nothing was left on the rock but one cone and two small sticks. Physics lesson number one: rapidly expanding gases produce enough force to blow light objects off a rock.

Cliff hurried around the rock to chase down any hot spots from the flaming needles, but after a few panicky moments, he'd found none. He settled down to let his leg recover. Plan A hadn't worked. Time for Plan B.

He moved back under the trees to gather more kindling. It was all over the place, so it wasn't hard to find, but it was painful and exhausting since he'd been without food for so long and had the leg wound. When his bindle was full, he returned to the rock. It took him half an hour to build another stable pile.

This time he wasn't going to try to ignite the tinder with the blast. He'd use the hot shell casing. That had ignited the needles before. The trick was to get it onto the pile quickly enough. It would cool rapidly in the morning air and there was no way to aim where it landed. He took a T-shirt from the bindle and thrust his gun hand into it so that the barrel of the gun protruded through the neck hole. The body of the shirt surrounded the gun and would serve as a net to catch the ejecting bullet.

He was afraid that the cloth would jam the gun's mechanism or get caught when the action closed and that would delay getting the hot shell out. So with his left hand he lifted the cloth up clear of the breech as he fingered the trigger with his right. This time he pointed the gun directly into the water, the deepest spot he could see. It was still not deep and he knew there could be a rock under the water presenting the risk of ricochet, but the risk of wildfire would be reduced. Once again he pulled the trigger.

The T-shirt worked more or less as intended, stopping the shell casing from flying off. Instead it was corralled by the fabric and fell down, rolling out of the shirt and hitting Cliff's knee before landing on the ground. Cliff pulled the gun from the shirt and used the shirt as a potholder to protect his fingers from burning. It took him thirty seconds to find the shell. His lost glasses were cursing him once again. If he'd had his glasses, he would have spotted the shell immediately. Then, if he'd had an ATV, he could drive out of here. If wishes were horses and all that. You had to work with what you had. He did finally find the shell and lifted it using the shirt. He dropped the shell into the tinder pile and began to blow on it. He could tell from the heat coming through the cloth that it was still hot when dropped in, but was it hot enough?

Wisps of smoke appeared. Cliff blew harder. Some needles glowed orange at their tips. More blowing; more glowing. Then it all cooled down. No more orange. Blowing harder had no effect. He reached in and pulled the shell casing out. It was still hot enough to burn his fingers. Physics lesson number two: human fingers experience pain at a temperature lower than that needed to ignite dry pine needles.

Cliff didn't have a Plan C. He was encouraged by this last attempt, even though it hadn't completely succeeded. There had been smoke. He wasn't ready to give up on Plan B. Cliff suddenly remembered the book he had ditched. If only he had those pages now, he was sure he could start a fire.

The dry canyon opened onto a valley to the east, but straight ahead was another canyon heading due north. The survivor might have gone either direction.

"He's been going downhill the whole way. I mean that literally, although figuratively might work, too. I think he'd turn east here and head for the trees down below, but we can't ignore the route straight ahead. Why don't you two follow that until you reach the first bend. If you don't see any sign of him, come back and go down this way. Meet me at the trees. If you don't meet me in an hour, I'll come back up and follow your route." It was Darryl giving the instructions.

There was some discussion, but Randy and Trish quickly agreed and headed up the canyon straight ahead. Darryl turned and headed east into the valley. He made his way slowly down the creekbed focused closely on the ground and surrounding scrub. Now that there were only two eyes instead of six, it was easier to miss something.

Twenty-two minutes later the beat of a helicopter sounded in the distance. He looked up as the sound got louder. He had the contact number of the observer in the helicopter. A satellite phone was allocated to that role. He dialed it. A woman answered. Darryl assumed it was the FBI agent who was being dropped at the crash site, the aviation specialist.

"Zaira."

"This is Darryl. You're in the copter?"

"Yep. You on one of the ground teams? Oh, Darryl. I see you on the personnel list. Have you had any luck?"

"Not yet. I hear you approaching. You'll be over me any second. We split up. The other two went north to check out that canyon running north. I headed downstream to the east. Are you the aviation specialist from L.A.?"

"No, we dropped him off already. I'm just here as an observer to help look. I'm from the FBI's Reno office."

"Good to have you with us." The helicopter banked into view to Darryl's left. He waved, but couldn't see any response. "I just saw you go by. I'm to your left and a little behind now. I'm waving."

"Okay, I see you now. You think he came this way?"

"I'm not sure, but I think so. You can do me a favor. Fly back up the valley and make a right where the canyon splits off north. We came from the south. My other team members should be up that way, either continuing north or heading back toward me. If they haven't found anything, they'll be coming back. If they found something they don't have a way to contact me. I've got the only satphone. If they're headed north, that means they found something and I'll go catch up with them. Call me back and let me know either way."

"You got it."

He could hear her give directions to the pilot. The helicopter turned to head up the valley and the aircraft quickly disappeared from view. It should be at the fork within five minutes max, he figured. After six minutes, he still hadn't heard from Zaira, so he called her. He would have liked to keep the line open, but satphone charges were horrendous.

"I'm here."

"You should see two figures. A man and a woman. Have you spotted them?"

"Well, I'm looking at one figure right now."

"One? They split up? Is it the man or the woman."

"Yes," she laughed. "Definitely."

"Sorry? I didn't get that. The person you see, is it a man, Asian?"

"It is. And a woman. I saw two people, but you asked if I saw two figures. They made only one figure. You couldn't get a piece of paper between them." She laughed again. "Okay, now they're coming apart. I was waiting to see which direction they were going. They weren't going anywhere a minute ago. Now they're waving to us. She's tucking in her shirt. He's pointing back toward you. It looks like they're headed your way."

"Okay, thanks." Darryl continued on down to the copse of trees shaking his head. He had not pegged those two as a likely couple. The helicopter could be heard in the distance turning away and heading east again.

When Trish and Randy reached the copse thirty minutes later, Darryl was waving to them to hurry up.

"It's a book! Look at this." Darryl was as excited as a puppy on ecstasy. "It's not weathered. This was left here recently."

"He was here," Randy added.

"Thank you, Captain Obvious," Trish said with a grin. "What's that thing?" She pointed to something dark and metallic barely visible under a bush.

Darryl picked it up and held it for the other two to see. It was the spare ammo magazine Cliff had jettisoned.

"Bullets! He's got a gun," Trish blurted out.

"Thank you, Lieutenant Obvious," Randy retorted. Trish hit him on the shoulder.

"He's lightening his load," Darryl said. "This is not good. He must be getting very tired. But at least he was alive to this point and could keep going. We're on the right track."

Trish replied, "But where did he get the gun? And why would he keep it without bullets? It must be heavy. Look around. Maybe it's here somewhere." She started scouring the area.

"One of them had the gun in the plane," Darryl answered. "They were FBI agents. I forgot to tell you. We found the empty gun case at the crash site. I'm pretty sure that's a spare magazine. There was a slot for one in the case and it was empty. He probably still has a loaded gun. Maybe he knew someone was after him, or maybe he just wanted to be able to signal to rescuers. A gun's not a bad idea."

"Up in the canyon the risk would be acceptable. There's nothing but rocks," Randy said. "But down here we have stands of trees and parched shrubs. It's all totally dry. Shooting could start a fire."

"All the more reason we need to find him fast." Darryl pulled out the satellite phone and dialed Forster. Forster had a satellite phone, too. Darryl filled him in on finding the book and ammo clip. They discussed the finding for a few minutes and concluded that the survivor was heading toward Glass Creek and was therefore somewhere between the two groups of searchers. If they continued converging, they should reach him eventually. If they got lucky, it could be in a few hours. If not, they might have to call for evacuation before nightfall. They couldn't search in the dark or stay the night in the mountains.

They were making slow progress because they had to search the ground thoroughly. They couldn't assume the survivor was conscious, or even alive, for that matter. He might have a gun and be able to signal his location that way, but that was no guarantee, either. After searching the area near the location of the book and ammo clip, the three found a few more discarded items, but nothing that helped them. At least they knew he'd found a good water source. He would stick near the stream. They filled their own bottles and took the time to purify it with filtration and a UV light purifier. They all knew hikers who hadn't and who'd ended up with giardia or some other infection. Then they began moving down the stream, calling Cliff's name.

On the fifth try Cliff succeeded in getting a fire started on the rock. He'd decided that it would be the last try. He only had three more bullets and he would need those to signal to any rescuers he heard. Possibly, he might need to defend himself against another assassin, although he discounted that possibility.

The little pile of cones and needles burned cleanly. It was also burning faster than he'd anticipated. Cliff could smell the smoke, but he couldn't see it, not more than a few wisps. Now that he'd started it, he needed it to grow and be visible. He needed to stoke the fire, but his limited mobility made that difficult. He managed to quickly gather another handful of needles and cones and get back in position to feed them to the flame. He placed a cone on top of the pile and it burst into flame immediately. This new fuel wasn't going to last long. He dumped the rest onto the pile and moved down to the water's edge. There leaves from the small bushes had formed a mat of dead vegetation carpeting the mud. He realized he needed wet leaves to make visible smoke. He scraped up a handful of the sticky layer and returned to the rock.

The fire was getting low already. He lay the damp leaf layer onto the flames. Dark smoke began to rise. He blew on it and the smoke volume increased. He repeated the process, this time adding more damp leaves. For a few moments the dark smoke rose in larger, darker billows. Then the smoke died down. Cliff blew on the pile, and the flames burned hotter again, but he realized he'd almost put it out. He repeated the process of adding more dry tinder. He got back to the fire as it died to a smolder. The fresh needles caught fire and restored life, but without the dark smoke. Once more he added damp leaves and the dark smoke rose again. On the third round of this dry/damp cycle he added too many damp leaves. He blew just as he had before, but it made little difference. He blew harder, but that only caused some of the remaining needles to fly off into the stream.

He rushed to gather up more dry needles and scrambled back to the rock. He dropped the new fuel onto the dwindling pile. It just sat there. He blew and blew, but there was no ignition. He'd put the fire out with the wet leaves. His heart sank. He was resolved not to use up his last bullets. Plan B had failed and he had no Plan C. He just had to hope they found him.

Ten miles away on the other side of Highway 395 a spotter in the fire tower noticed something, something that could be smoke or a dust cloud. He radioed the CalFire captain covering the area and reported that there appeared to be possible smoke on San Joaquin Mountain. He was also aware that a recovery operation was underway for the plane crash victims that had been located. He was not aware that there was a survivor. His only concern at that point was for the possibility of a fire and the safety of the SAR crew. He called the county 911 operator and advised them of the possibility.

The operator, aware of the rescue operation in progress, radioed Deputy Forster. Forster called the fire tower directly from his satellite phone.

"Tower seven."

"This is Forster with Mono Sheriff. I'm leading the search operation in the area where you spotted smoke."

"You're recovering the bodies from the plane crash?"

"We recovered one body already. We're on a search and rescue for the survivor. That smoke could have been a signal to us. We need a pinpoint location if possible."

"There's a survivor? Hell, if I'd known that … hold on." After a few moments he came back on. "It's gone. It was only there for a minute or two. Probably less. I didn't take a bearing reading. There wasn't time. I'm trying to picture it in my mind again. It's possibly around the midline between June Lake and the summit of San Joaquin Mountain looking from my tower."

"How near or far?"

"No way to tell. Well past – that is, west – of 395. That's all I can say for sure."

"How sure are you it was smoke?"

"Hmm, not sure, but it looked like smoke to me. Sometimes dust devils send a little spiral of debris up in the air. Those can fool you. I'm sorry I didn't get a reading for you. I can keep focused on that area as much as possible for the next hour or so, but I have to cover three hundred sixty degrees."

“Sure. Anything you can do.” He gave the fire tower operator his satellite phone number and ended the call.

He summarized the call for his assembled crew members then continued. “The location description he gave us covers pretty much our whole search area. That doesn’t help us. But the key here is that it’s a sign he could be alive and actively trying to attract attention. I’m guessing, based on the tower’s guess, that the area is about three or four miles to our west southwest. There will be some serious rock climbs that way unless we go the long way around following the creek, which isn’t easy either. We’d be lucky to get there by nightfall if we had an exact location. Without one, we’ll have to follow the creek. That’s still the most likely way he’d go, or where he’d settle in.”

After some internal discussion, the group resumed its trek up the creek.

Chapter 20

The sun's brutality continued throughout the day. Cliff continually moved to stay in the shade, but he was too weak to go far. He crabwalked around the large tree nearest the creek to be in its shade. Then he made his way back to the creek to refill his water bottle. He had no food.

This back and forth had gone on most of the day. By 5:30 the sun was well below the western mountains, so there was shade everywhere. Cliff parked himself by the creek and minimized his movement to save energy. It was then that he heard the helicopter for the third time. It was the first time it had flown within his view. It glided by almost directly overhead.

He stood and waved, then watched in despair as it continued on its way without any sign he'd been seen. He knew how hard it was to spot something in deep shade on the ground when you're up above in bright sunlight. He'd done airborne surveillance a few times in his career. What may seem like a large movement on the ground, like an arm waving, is dwarfed compared to faster, grander movements like treetops swaying, or a cluster of tumbleweeds blowing along the ground at twenty miles an hour. Those are what catch the eye.

Despite the letdown when the helicopter didn't come back, he didn't become discouraged. At least they were looking for him, and they were looking in the right area. He had water. He just needed to hold out until they found him. By nightfall his hunger pangs were more intense and he'd given up hope of rescue today. His best hope was to be able to sleep and keep his fingers crossed for tomorrow.

The smell from Bui's body was making that difficult. Vultures and other birds had already made considerable progress on the body. Cliff had watched them land and leave. Some small creatures of the night were nosing around there now. Cliff heard them, but didn't know what they were and didn't want to know. He'd moved far enough away that he could no longer see the corpse, so he didn't have to watch any of them fill their bellies, whether birds or beasts. The cold was setting in.

He curled up in his space blanket and closed his eyes.

The disappointment was as bad as her high school senior ball night when she had sat home alone crying in her room. No one had asked her. Trish had hinted strongly to a boy she didn't even like all that much, but who she thought at least didn't have a girlfriend. He'd told her he wasn't going to the dance and avoided her after that. Now it was another night of being hauled away in a helicopter with the victim alone out in the wilderness. She and Randy and Darryl had marked their progress and would resume tomorrow, but they'd come only about two miles from Forster's team. Another hour of searching and they'd have converged. They must have been close. It hurt to abandon the search, but it was too dark and dangerous to continue.

Randy was disappointed, too, but for him it was like when he'd washed out of the Seal Team tryouts in San Diego. He knew it had been his ego that had been hurt then, but now it was someone's life. He was more mature now. He could swallow his pride, but he knew he'd agonize for the rest of his life if it turned out they'd come within a mile of the victim and he'd died tonight after they'd gone. Darryl had told him more about this Cliff Knowles fellow during the day. "The survivor" had become a human. He was a retired FBI agent, now a private eye. He'd found the San Quentin killer. He had a wife and two children, young children despite the fact he wasn't young. He was a contributing human being, one of the good guys, and deserved saving. Sure, technically everyone did, but to him it made a difference.

The search effort had grown larger. Many volunteers had called to help and a few even showed up, but almost all of them had to be turned away. There were no trails. This was dangerous terrain and searchers had to be fit and trained. The command post had been set up in the June Mountain Ski Area parking lot. The helicopters could land there. Both ground teams were now assembled there. The Sheriff had made arrangements to find lodging nearby for all his personnel and the SAR team members. Mono County SAR Members who hadn't been turned out for the original recovery effort were now present and being briefed. Two U.S. Forest Rangers were now in the group.

The FBI team from Fresno with the thermal imaging equipment were here, too. Their helicopter was a Huey, capable of carrying thirteen passengers, although it wasn't configured that way. They had brought a crew of six, including two pilots, but could manage ten in a pinch.

The FBI team would search overnight with the thermal imaging gear. If nothing was found, the regular ground teams would start in the morning from three different points. This was necessitated by the fact that Duc Bui, aka Doug, had never returned to the parking area. His car sat there unoccupied and apparently never touched overnight. He was now officially a missing person, too. He had last been known to be heading back down the same route the team had taken two days earlier. One of the three teams would have to start at the same point and hike up that way. Since Darryl had led the team on that route originally, he would take that crew. One of the FBI agents, a SWAT team member, would be part of that team since there was a possibility that Bui could be armed and hostile.

The Huey didn't have a winch and rappelling gear, so it couldn't drop Randy's team, but there was a landing spot near where Forster's team had left off the previous day, so they'd carry that team in. Forster was armed and would lead one team from there. Randy and Trish would lead one team from their previous spot, along with one other FBI agent, also armed. The sheriff's helicopter would have to make another trip after dropping them. It would deposit the NTSB investigator at the crash site along with an aviation investigator, and only then begin searching visually for the survivor.

Once the Huey had dropped off the ground team, it, too, would help with the visual search. The daytime flying would be done by the second FBI pilot since the one who flew the night shift would need to sleep during the day. The two helicopters would split up the territory to cover.

This plan was conveyed to everyone present. Some stragglers arrived late and got the word passed down by word of mouth. People began to filter away. They all wanted to get to bed early and be up early enough to take advantage of all the daylight.

The civilian volunteers who couldn't be included in the search itself were put to good use. They helped shuttle team members and their gear to and from the local lodging, including the homes of some local residents who'd volunteered their use. Others had brought food, tables, canopies, folding chairs, extra clothing, first aid kits, and similar items. A few hardy souls agreed to stay overnight in the parking lot in their campers or trailers in case the Huey crew spotted something and a night-time rescue was initiated.

The Huey crew leader took the first night shift and designated a pilot and second observer. The stragglers watched as the impressive craft lifted off and headed toward the search area soon after sundown. The night vision equipment used infrared or IR radiation to detect heat sources. The electronics were sensitive to that range of the light spectrum that is invisible to the human eye.

It had one drawback in this situation: it worked best in a cold environment and this was a very hot area. It was still over 90 degrees at ground level when they took off. There were many hot spots on the ground as hot as, or hotter than, a human being. A warm body wouldn't register an image if it was close to the same temperature as the surrounding ground. Even so, at this altitude and time of year the ground cooled quite rapidly. It would be plenty cold enough by 9:30 or so. They expected to be searching most of the night and going over the same area repeatedly, so it didn't matter if the first few minutes weren't the best search conditions.

The crew flew to the starting corner of the search grid and proceeded to fly in a north-south alternating pattern, much like a crop duster, slowly moving westward. At 1:17 AM it passed within forty yards of Cliff's position. The observers saw nothing out of the ordinary below and continued on. When it reached the western side of the Sierras at the far corner of the search grid, it turned eastward and began covering the same rectangle in an east-west pattern.

Cliff was in a deep slumber when the Huey's first pass came by. At first he thought it was a dream. After a few moments, his brain registered the reality. He turned over in his Mylar cocoon and looked up. He could see the helicopter's lights moving slowly westward through the night sky, the body eclipsing the stars one by one. By the time he was awake enough to take in the situation fully, the Huey was passing out of sight to the west.

They didn't see me, was his first thought. *Of course they didn't see me. It's the middle of the night. It's hard enough to spot someone in a forest during the daytime. There was no chance to succeed at night. What are those idiots doing?*

He was encouraged that they were still looking, and in the right area. If he was still alive by the morning, something that seemed to be getting less likely by the hour, there was a chance he'd be found. He was shivering from the cold. He hadn't taken in enough calories to keep himself warm. He thought about putting on one more layer from his bindle. *There's another T-shirt in there, but that won't do me much good. I'll stick with the space blanket.*

He wrapped himself even tighter in the blanket and tried to get back to sleep, but his brain was too active. The helicopter had spurred an adrenaline surge. As he lay there fighting his own hormonal system, a note of recognition crept into his brain. The sound. It wasn't the same helicopter as before. But he's heard that peculiar *whap whap whap* before. It's a Huey! He'd ridden in one back in the FBI.

So they've brought in another helicopter. Why? And why search at night? He finally made the connection. *Thermal imaging. They're trying to spot me from my heat signature! But then, why didn't they? Or did they? Are they coming back?*

These thoughts and more raced through his mind for an hour as he lay there. There was no way he was going back to sleep now. There must be something he could do to make himself more visible. The battery on his own phone was dead and the one on Bui's phone was too low. He'd turned it off. He could try turning it on and using the flashlight app if the Huey came by again, but would they be able to see it? If they were using thermal imaging, they would not see the visible light. If it was night vision equipment, the flashlight might be blinding, but it would work. The problem with that was he had no way to know when it would return. He'd drain the battery if he kept it on waiting, and if it was off when the Huey came by, he might not have enough time to unlock it and get the flashlight working. He needed that email to go out with the video of Bui naming Dice for the Tran murder. If he used the other phone, the one from the first aid kit, it, too, had a very low battery. If he drained it down to nothing shining it into the sky, then he'd have no working lifeline.

The gun! I could shoot the gun. The barrel gets very hot when a round is fired. It'll stand out like fireworks to thermal imaging. But I only have three rounds left.

Cliff knew he would need one or two rounds to shoot the next day if a ground search crew got near. None of this logic puzzle would matter unless the Huey came by again. He made sure the gun was ready to fire and sat shivering, wrapped in his space blanket, waiting for another pass of his savior on high.

That moment came ninety-four minutes later. Cliff heard the sound well before its lights signaled its presence. He could tell the direction wasn't the same as before. It was at a right angle. This made sense to him. They were crisscrossing the search area. He took the gun in hand and watched as the helicopter lumbered slowly toward him over the mountain crest. He fired it into the pitch blackness at what he hoped was forest on the far side of the creek.

In the Huey the three crew members had their individual duties. One observer sat on the right side and was responsible for watching the ground ahead and to the right. The other observer did the same on the left side. The pilot's job was to fly the helicopter. This last might sound too obvious to mention, but one would be surprised at how often aircraft accidents happen because the pilot was distracted by other things. The pilot wasn't there to search the ground. He needed to keep an eye on the instruments and the general eye-level terrain so that he didn't fly into a mountain or an unusually tall tree. He couldn't see the ground features well enough for night navigation, so he had to keep the copter above the altitude of the tallest mountain in the search area. He also had to maintain communications and watch out for other aircraft, although at this time and location there was little chance of there being any.

Each observer was equipped with two technologies: night vision and thermal imaging. The two were often confused. They were not interchangeable. Thermal imaging didn't need visible light. In fact, it didn't work very well in broad daylight, at least not for finding a human body, because the sun made many things as warm or warmer than a human body. At night, the heat from a mammal's body stands out clearly against a cold earth background.

Night vision equipment, on the other hand, required visible light. It didn't require much, but it needed at least a little. It worked by amplifying very weak light. The user wore special goggles that were sensitive to the low light and enhanced it so that the wearer could see it. A very bright light could be painfully blinding to a user and damage some models. It worked best in an urban environment where there is almost always ambient light, or, if outside in a rural area, when the moon is out. Tonight there was no moon, but the sky was clear and there was some starlight. The observers were mostly using thermal imaging, but every now and then they would switch to night vision in hopes that Cliff might have a flashlight, campfire, or other light source to signal them. Although the night vision scope had a narrow field of vision, it had the advantage of being able to detect a light at a considerable distance in these conditions. Thermal imaging had a more limited range.

As the Huey approached Cliff's site, it would pass so that Cliff was on the left. As luck would have it, at the moment Cliff fired the gun, the observer on the right was looking to the right with his thermal imaging viewer and didn't see the hot metal on the opposite side. The observer on the left had switched to night vision equipment right before the shot and was looking dead ahead while Cliff's position was to the left at a ten o'clock position. He didn't see the muzzle flash and it wasn't bright enough to light up the landscape where he was looking. The pilot was looking dead ahead. The shot wasn't loud enough to penetrate the Huey's rotor noise and the observers' ear protectors. The result was that the helicopter flew on by with none of the three noticing anything.

The flash of the gun had a major disadvantage: it was momentary. Unless the observer was looking the right direction at that instant, it did no good, especially with the narrow field of vision of the night vision scope. The light was gone instantly. The left side observer switched back to thermal imaging only thirty seconds after sweeping with the night vision scope. The heat of the gun barrel lasted many minutes. It would have stood out like Rudolph's nose on Christmas night had the observer been looking that way, but by then the helicopter had moved past. Cliff was behind them, out of view.

By the time the Huey had completed its second full pass over the search grid, it was low on fuel and had to return to Mammoth-Yosemite Airport. After it refueled, it was getting close to sunrise. The crew debated whether to keep searching or return to the command center to turn things over to the daytime crew.

After some discussion, they decided that the ground was still cold and dark enough that the thermal imaging and night vision was useful and they still had almost an hour of legal flight time for the pilot. So they set off for a third pass, intending to cut it short when the sun came up.

Cliff had been tormented with questions when the Huey had passed over him on its second pass. *Why didn't it see me? It should have seen the muzzle flash and the heat of the barrel.* But there was nothing he could do about it. He'd resumed shivering in his space blanket trying to get some sleep. His body was having a hard time maintaining his body temperature. If he could just make it until dawn, he could lie in the sun and hope the search continued.

He got no sleep. His ears were by now attuned to the incessant sound of the helicopter's rotors and heard them constantly, even when there was nothing to be heard. He'd developed a mechanical earworm that he thought would drive him crazy. So he refused to believe his ears when the sound grew louder and louder. His will to survive overcame his self-doubt and he opened his eyes. The sky was growing lighter.

He sat up, still shivering. The sound was real, he realized. The copter was coming over again. He had little time to think. He grabbed the gun and then dropped it. It hadn't worked before, so he had no reason to think it would work the second time. He stood and watched as the Huey appeared over the ridge headed directly for him.

In the helicopter the left side observer was using thermal imaging. As he swept forward, he saw a bright spot. "Hey, look straight ahead. There's something moving."

The other observer directed his thermal scope that direction. "Yeah, I see it. It's too small to be a person. Maybe a porcupine or possum." The image in the scope had no resolution like a camera or binoculars would have. At this distance, thousands of feet up, it didn't show the shape beyond a very rough, fuzzy silhouette. In this case, it looked more or less circular.

"It's a mammal at least. We haven't seen many. Can you take us down a little?"

The pilot hovered for a moment and descended.

"No, you're right. It's too small to be him. Take it back up."

The Huey began to rise.

Down below, Cliff was elated at first. The Huey had stopped and appeared to come down a little. They must have spotted him. He stood and waved one hand. But it had begun to rise again. He was perplexed. Had they seen him or not?

His calorie-starved brain hadn't completely lost its inherent intelligence. Dredging from somewhere deep in his experience and education, it was calling out, trying to tell him something important. He was missing something. If only he could think!

Then it hit him. The space blanket! It was designed to block IR radiation. That was its whole point, the reason for its design. Its Mylar layer was a mirror to infrared, reflecting the rays back inside for warmth, preventing their escape. If the Huey was using thermal imaging technology, they would see nothing but the oval of his face.

He threw off the blanket and peeled off the jacket he wore underneath. He stood and waved, hopping on his good leg. He watched as the Huey continued to rise.

In the helicopter the reaction was instant. "Hang on! Did you see that? It just got bigger," one of the observers exclaimed. The image of the creature below had grown in size tenfold. And it was animated. "Go back down."

Within thirty seconds the copter crew had confirmed it was a person signaling to them. The pilot maneuvered as low as he could, but the conifers here were too tall to allow it to get close enough for a rescue. There was no place to land and the Huey wasn't equipped with a harness and cable. It was designed for surveillance and transport, not search and rescue. One of the observers tossed a packet of protein bars and a first aid kit on the ground near Cliff and gave a thumbs up but Cliff was unable to see it since there was no illumination from below. He heard the protein bars hit nearby. It was just beginning to get light enough for him to make out shapes on ground. He found one of the bars and picked it up.

The pilot had already radioed that they located the survivor and read off the coordinates to the command post and the entire search team. It was the open channel everyone used. The sheriff's helicopter was already in the air, just starting its shift. It radioed back that it was on the way. Much as the FBI crew would have liked to be the ones to rescue one of their own, they knew the Sheriff's helicopter was better equipped for that task. They moved away to give the airspace over to the other craft.

Cliff ripped open a protein bar and bit off a chunk. It tasted like manna from heaven and in a way it was. His brain fog was clearing rapidly either from the sugar or the adrenaline. His gloom disappeared despite seeing the Huey fly away. It was obvious to him what had occurred. His position had been marked. That helicopter wasn't able to pick him up, but he was sure rescue was right around the corner. He gathered up all his stuff and wrapped it in the space blanket again.

Twenty minutes later the Mono County search and rescue helicopter appeared overhead. The helicopter hovered safely above the treetops directly over his position. Randy Whiting descended in a harness, but reached the end of the cable still sixty feet in the air. The aircraft couldn't get any closer at this point due to the trees. Randy signaled to be brought back up. Several minutes later he was lowered to the ground further downstream in a more open area where the helicopter could get closer to the ground. Randy quickly made his way up to Cliff's position through the trees.

"You must be Cliff," he said when they finally came face to face.

"Guilty as charged. I'm sure glad to see you, whoever you are."

"Randy. I'm with Mono County Search and Rescue. Are you injured?"

"A twisted ankle and a gunshot wound in my leg. That's going to need attention."

"How'd you get shot?"

Cliff turned his head and nodded toward Bui's body. It was downwind from their position and fifty or so yards away, so the smell wasn't obvious, but when Randy strode over toward the corpse, he quickly reversed his course. He said nothing to Cliff about the body.

"You have any more of those candy bars?" Cliff asked. It had tasted so sweet to him he'd mistaken it for candy.

Randy handed him another protein bar and a juice box like moms pack in their kids' lunchboxes. Cliff finished both off in a matter of seconds. "Can you walk?" Randy asked.

Cliff ignored the question. "He tried to kill me. I think he's part of a gang …"

"Save it," Randy interrupted. "I know who he is. His name is Doug Bui and he was hunting you. I'm a civilian, not law enforcement. I'm deputized for search and rescue only. Tell it to the homicide people when we get back. I don't want to get involved and be a witness to what you said. Now can you walk?"

"With your help, probably."

"Let's get you out of here." He got Cliff on his feet and tried a few steps. It wasn't going to be easy, but he judged that Cliff could make it to the downstream spot where he'd been dropped off. He pulled a two-way radio off his belt and spoke to the helicopter pilot. "The crash survivor is alive. We're going to go to where you let me down. I'll send him up in the harness. He needs medevac, but it's not critical. I'll stay behind for now. There's a dead body. Have the sheriff send someone to secure the scene and deal with the body. It's that Bui guy. You can scratch that search."

The helicopter pilot acknowledged and Cliff heard it move downstream again. It had moved directly overhead after lowering Randy. He and Randy started moving again and it was all Cliff could do not to call out in pain, but he held it in. If he'd been home with Ellen he'd have been whining shamelessly, but the guy code was applicable in this situation. He was supposed to be a tough FBI guy in public.

"Get my stuff. The crap in the space blanket is mine. I need my phone and his phone, too. There's another one, too. He was using it to track the plane. It was stashed in the first aid kit."

Randy hesitated a moment. He wasn't sure if that would be disturbing a crime scene. Then he told himself the hell with it, the shooting was going to be self-defense anyway. If Cliff wanted his stuff, he was going to get his stuff. He propped Cliff against a tree with a low branch Cliff could grab so that his weight could be partially taken off his leg. Then he went back and grabbed the bindle.

Twenty minutes later they were at the pickup point. Cliff was strapped in without difficulty and hauled up, bindle in hand. Trish was there in the helicopter bay with a first aid kit open. In addition to the pilot, a white male with the logo of the sheriff's office on his sleeve, there was a black woman with an FBI logo on her T-shirt.

"Cliff, I'm Zaira, Sacramento Division. This is Trish. She's going to take care of your leg. This is a federal case now. Do you mind answering a few questions?" She held up her phone with a questioning look.

"Go ahead. You can record me." She punched the video record icon. He noticed she had a sniper rifle by her foot. That's why the helicopter had moved back into position after dropping off Randy. She'd been prepared to pick off Bui or anyone else who was lying in wait. Trish began cleaning and dressing his wound. He felt the prick of a needle in his thigh, then it went numb from a local anesthetic. Trish handed him a sedative and a water bottle. He swallowed the pill.

"What do you remember about the plane crash?" Zaira asked.

"We were flying home normally. At least it seemed normal to me until Jim said something was wrong with the fuel gauge. Then he said 'Brace for impact.' That's the last thing I remember until I woke up in the crashed plane. Jim was dead. A branch had speared right through him."

"Do you remember what he said about the fuel?"

"Not really. Just the gauge was malfunctioning, I think."

"Were you injured in the crash?"

"Not much. Bruises from the seat belt. A nasty scratch on one leg when I climbed out and I was coughing from the smoke. I probably got some bad fumes in my lungs. I don't know how I survived unscathed and Jim didn't. He did an amazing job hitting that burned out tree. I didn't realize it until afterward, but that's what saved my life. The tree slowed the plane just enough."

"Tell me about what happened here. The gunshot wound."

Cliff gave a long, uninterrupted account of Bui's approach, the gunfight, how he'd searched the body and taken the ammunition, and everything else he thought would be relevant to the criminal case. She didn't ask, and he didn't volunteer, anything about his trek from the crash site and his efforts to find food and water.

"You have a recording of him naming Dice as killing Raven? Did I hear that right?"

"Right. I recorded it on his phone. My phone battery ran out, so I used his."

"That's interstate travel, too. And no statute of limitations on murder. If we can't nail him on plane sabotage or the Las Vegas case, we've got him on that. Your wife's an agent in San Francisco Division, isn't she?"

"Yes, but she can't be involved in a case involving me as a victim. Does she know I've been rescued?"

"Yes. The pilot told command you were being hauled up. They called her. You can talk to her as soon as we land."

Trish spoke for the first time. "You're going to be taken to Fresno to get checked out. There are some closer hospitals, but they aren't as well-equipped. You're stable enough and it will be easier for your wife to meet you there."

"We have to get the Huey back there anyway," Zaira added. "We might as well save you and your insurance the cost of a medevac ride. They'll probably keep you overnight for observation."

"Yeah, my wife can drive to Fresno."

"This helicopter doesn't have the range for that. We're going to land at June Lake and transfer you to the Huey. We should be there soon."

Trish was taking his pulse. He started getting drowsy and realized that the pill she'd given him was taking effect. He was vaguely aware that Zaira was on the radio talking to someone, giving a shortened version of what he'd told her.

The helicopter set down gently in the ski lodge parking lot. He noticed people nearby were talking on their cell phones. There must be cell coverage here. That reminded him to send the video he had on Bui's phone. He asked Zaira to get it from the bindle and hand it to him. There were three phones there. His own was identifiable by its holder. The other two phones looked identical, and he wasn't sure which one was Bui's and which the one from the first aid kit.

"Let me try those two," he said, pointing to the ones that weren't his.

"Which one is yours?"

"The other one. I want to see Bui's phone for a second."

"I can't give that to you now that it's in FBI custody. You understand chain of custody."

"I don't need to touch it. Just turn it on. Turn both of them on."

"Why?"

"The video I told you about. I sent it as an attachment, but I had no cell service so it hasn't gone out yet. As soon as you turn it on, I think it will send automatically and I'll get it on my phone and so will Ellen. Then it'll be in FBI possession."

"It's in FBI possession now."

"But not accessible. Go ahead; try to view it."

Zaira thought about that for a few seconds. There was no rule or policy she could think of that prevented her from turning it on. She was an investigator and could examine evidence, although normally phones were turned over to tech trained agents. She turned on the two burner phones. After a few seconds they both came on.

"They're locked," she announced needlessly.

"That's the point. You can't view the video unless you can unlock the phone. I need the video to go out as an attachment so we … you … can use it."

"I don't know if we can unlock it. Some phone's security can't be broken. I've turned it on. If you're right that it would send automatically, then you can just check your own phone and the video should be there."

"My phone has zero charge. I won't be able to check it until we get to some place where I can charge it, or get to a computer with Internet access. I need to see if the email was sent."

"Well, they're both locked, like I said. I can't access them right now."

"I can," Cliff replied impatiently.

"You know his password? Just tell me and I'll enter it."

"I don't know his password. Just hand me the phones."

Zaira was still hesitant and started to say something but Cliff cut her off. "Okay, you keep them. Just hold them both up facing you so I can see the backs."

She didn't understand, but saw no harm in this so she did. At least he might be able to identify which phone was Bui's. Cliff reached out and touched his forefinger to the ovals on the back of both phones. The one in Zaira's right hand instantly unlocked and displayed the home screen. Zaira let out a small gasp of surprise.

"You unlocked it! How'd you do that?"

"Let me see," he directed. Zaira turned the phone toward him. The email app was open on the screen. He saw his email with the video attachment queued up and ready to send. He touched the send icon and the email disappeared from the screen. "When I took the phone from him, I unlocked it with his finger. He was dead, but it still worked. While the phone was still unlocked I added my fingerprint to the security settings. These phones usually allow at least two prints, just in case the first one doesn't work. I can unlock mine with my right hand or my left."

"Why not just change the password?"

"I'd rather use the fingerprint method."

Then it dawned on Zaira what he'd done and why. She smiled admiringly. "You sneaky bastard. You knew we'd take the phone, or the police would. You wanted to be the only one who could unlock it. When we examine it, you wanted to be able to be there and see what's on it."

"No, not really, but you're close. I just anticipated this situation right here. I wanted to be able to be sure the email got sent. Now I have to call my wife and let her know I'm okay. She's going to get a copy of that email and not know what it is."

"Here, use mine," Trish said with a defiant glare at Zaira. "It's not evidence." She handed him her phone.

Cliff dialed Ellen's number but the line was busy. She was on the line with Maeva. If she'd known it was him, she would have taken the call waiting line, of course, but she didn't recognize Trish's number. Cliff left a voice mail telling her he was fine and was being taken to Fresno to be checked out. Then he hung up. By this point he was getting very sleepy, but he got out of the helicopter with the help of Trish on one arm and Zaira on the other.

Minutes later he found himself in the Huey helicopter and fell promptly asleep.

Chapter 21
Fresno, California

Maeva arrived at the hospital to find Zaira in the waiting room. They introduced themselves to each other. Zaira told her Cliff was having scans and other tests done, so she was unable to see him. Ellen showed up a few minutes later. After the heartfelt hugs, they settled down to wait for news.

The doctor who came out to talk to them was built like a medicine ball on a TV tray – all belly and spindly limbs. He told them Cliff had picked up an intestinal parasite and his leg wound was possibly infected. They were going to keep him overnight, maybe two, and treat him with antibiotics and anti-parasite drugs. He pronounced him out of danger and able to have visitors.

Zaira stayed in the waiting room while the others piled into Cliff's room and repeated the hugging with more vigor, this time with Cliff as the object. Cliff told Ellen and Maeva the whole story from start to finish from his perspective. Then Maeva filled in the gaps with what she'd learned in Las Vegas. Ellen told Cliff that she'd received the video Bui had made and forwarded it to the gang squad supervisor in San Jose. Traveling from one state to another to kill or intimidate a witness was an ITAR violation – Interstate Travel in Aid of Racketeering. That case would be rolling by the next day.

Cliff was soon inundated with phone calls, including several from reporters and from Melissa Ingram. He sent the first few to voice mail, but when the FBI Director called, he felt he had to take it. He gave an apologetic look to Ellen and Maeva, and they left the room. Ellen went out to check on the kids. Zaira assured Ellen that someone from the Fresno FBI office would drive Cliff home once he was released. Orders had come down the pipe from the Director's office to give Cliff the royal treatment. Ellen shouldn't have to make the three hundred mile round trip from the Bay Area again. Ellen thanked her for all she'd done and said she'd return home. Her sister had watched her kids enough already. Now that she knew Cliff was okay, it was time to get back to her life. Maeva felt the same way. They said their goodbyes and took off.

Four months later
Las Vegas

Transcript
INGRAM: Please state your name for record.

KNOWLES: Cliff Knowles.

INGRAM: How are you employed, Mr. Knowles?

KNOWLES: I run my own private investigation firm.

INGRAM: How were you employed eight years ago?

KNOWLES: I was a Special Agent of the Federal Bureau of Investigation.

INGRAM: An FBI agent. Impressive.

BOLLINGER: Objection.

INGRAM: I withdraw the remark. Mr. Knowles, are you familiar with the name Raven Tran?

KNOWLES: I am. Another agent and I arrested her eight years ago.

INGRAM: The other agent would be Mr. James Crosby, is that correct?

KNOWLES: That's right.

INGRAM: What was she arrested for?

KNOWLES: The arrest warrant was for what the FBI calls Unlawful flight – Murder. At the request of Las Vegas P.D. a federal warrant was issued for her in connection with the murder of Mr. Truong's brother-in-law, the victim in this case.

INGRAM: Mr. Knowles, I'd ask you to take a look at People's Exhibit 7. Do you recognize this?

KNOWLES: I do. That's a cassette tape recording Ms. Tran made after the arrest. Those are my initials on it along with those of Special Agent Crosby.

INGRAM: Did you ask Ms. Tran to make the recording?

KNOWLES: No. She asked us to record her statement. She was afraid Mr. Truong …

BOLLINGER: Objection. Hearsay. Speculation. Move to strike.

THE COURT: Sustained. Strike the response after the word statement. Mr. Knowles, please just answer the question as asked.

INGRAM: Were you present as the recording was made?

KNOWLES: I was.

INGRAM: Special Agent Knowles, please tell the jury, did you, Special Agent Crosby, or anyone put Ms. Tran under any form of duress during the making of the recording?

KNOWLES: No.

INGRAM: Do you know what happened to the recording after it was completed?

KNOWLES: Yes. Special Agent Crosby kept it in his possession until an officer from Las Vegas P.D. came to take Ms. Tran back. He handed the tape to the officer. That's standard procedure on an unlawful flight case.

INGRAM: Your honor, we've already heard from the officer who received the tape. I move that the tape be admitted into evidence.

BOLLINGER: I object, your honor. The tape is highly prejudicial hearsay.

INGRAM: Your honor, the court has reviewed the transcript of the recording. As you know, Ms. Tran makes serious admissions against her own penal interest. She's also a co-conspirator with Mr. Truong. Those are both exceptions to the hearsay rule. As for it being prejudicial, I think the adjective Mr. Bollinger is seeking is probative. That's what we call convincing evidence.

BOLLINGER: I can speak for myself. I'm saying …

THE COURT: Enough. I know you're both just making a record for appeal. I've heard all the arguments in the motions *in limine*. The tape has been authenticated. The hearsay exceptions apply. It's admitted into evidence. The clerk will mark it. The jury is instructed to ignore Ms. Ingram's remark about it being convincing evidence. It is your sole responsibility to judge the weight of the evidence.

INGRAM: I have no further questions. I would like to play the tape now.

[The tape recording is played for the jury]

THE COURT: Your witness, Mr. Bollinger.

BOLLINGER: Mr. Knowles, you make your living now as a hired gun, don't you?

INGRAM: Objection.

THE COURT: Sustained. You know better.

BOLLINGER: My apologies, your honor. I'll rephrase. Mr. Knowles, you aren't an FBI agent now, are you?

KNOWLES: No, sir. I'm retired from the FBI.

BOLLINGER: And when you were an agent, you were just an ordinary agent, weren't you?

INGRAM: Objection.

BOLLINGER: I'll rephrase. What I'm asking is, you call yourself a Special Agent when really all FBI agents are called Special Agents, isn't that right? So you aren't so special, are you?

INGRAM: Objection.

KNOWLES: It's okay, I can answer. Special Agents of the FBI are special. They're empowered by the U.S. Congress to carry firearms, to use deadly force if necessary, to execute arrest warrants and search warrants, to investigate all federal crimes, to administer oaths in civil cases, and to train and assist state and local law enforcement officers. I'd call that pretty special.

BOLLINGER: Did you administer Miranda warnings to Ms. Tran?

KNOWLES: Yes, Special Agent Crosby did.

BOLLINGER: You went to law school, didn't you?

KNOWLES: Yes.

BOLLINGER: Mr. Knowles, you testified that Ms. Tran confessed, isn't that right?

KNOWLES: That's true.

BOLLINGER: And as a trained attorney and FBI agent, you understood from what she said that she was guilty of murder, didn't you?

INGRAM: Objection. Best evidence rule. The tape speaks for itself. What Mr. Knowles remembers or understood her to say is irrelevant.

BOLLINGER: The witness is a lawyer and an expert in criminal law and confessions if he's as special as he says. Expert opinion is allowed in interpreting evidence.

THE COURT: I'll allow it. You may answer, Mr. Knowles.

KNOWLES: That's not clear. What she admitted to may or may not have been murder on her part. She admitted driving the getaway car. She knew the defendant was going to threaten the victim. That's definitely an admission of a criminal act. She knew the defendant came out afterward with a bloody knife in his hand. She didn't admit to knowing ahead of time that he was going to kill or harm the victim or that a murder had occurred until later. She might have been an accessory, but she might also have been under duress.

BOLLINGER: And as an expert, you know that criminals when confessing often try to shift the blame to others, don't you?

KNOWLES: I know that their attorneys do.

[disturbance in the courtroom]

THE COURT: The gallery is admonished that this is not a laughing matter. I will not tolerate another outburst like that. Anyone who finds themselves unable to control themselves should find another place to be.

BOLLINGER: I have no further questions.

THE COURT: Redirect?

INGRAM: No, your honor.

THE COURT: The witness is excused. Remain available until the trial has concluded.

End transcript

Cliff left the stand and waited in Ingram's office until the lunch break. When Melissa came in, she said Slonsky had finished testifying and the state had rested its case. Slonsky had already taken off, so she suggested the two of them have lunch in the cafeteria downstairs. Over a surprisingly good taco salad Cliff asked how it went.

"Very well. I don't know what Bollinger's going to do on defense. He could call you again, but I doubt he will. That final answer of yours cut him to the bone. It wasn't just the gallery that was laughing; several jurors were, too."

"Glad to be of service, ma'am," he replied, tipping an imaginary cowboy hat.

"Obviously he was trying to pin the murder on her instead of Dice. You were sharp to make the point that even if she didn't admit to murder, she admitted to a crime, so the hearsay exception for penal interest applied. I think he was hoping you wouldn't mention that and he could get the tape excluded after all. You didn't fall for it."

Ingram's phone buzzed. She took a look at a text. "It's Bollinger. He wants to know if my plea offer is still on the table. I told him before trial it wouldn't be once the jury was seated. He's obviously scared." She put the phone away without replying.

They spent the next twenty minutes eating and engaging in small talk. Suddenly there was a commotion. They looked around and saw that the diners were looking at one of the deputies who had rushed in, gun in hand. He was scanning the room frantically. Then he turned and left.

Ingram's phone buzzed again. It was another Bollinger text. She read it and grimaced. She turned the phone toward Cliff. The text read: "He shot a guard. I didn't know. Watch out."

A few seconds later two more deputies entered the dining room, guns out. They warned everyone that there was an active shooter and to stay put. One guard planted himself by the door while the other one went back into the serving area. There was an emergency exit at the other end of the room. Cliff looked that way. Some diners had approached that door, but another deputy was standing outside and waving them back. They retreated.

"I guess he got loose," Cliff said. "I don't think we're in any danger here."

The blare of sirens filled the air. Melissa said, "That deputy knows me. Let me see what I can find out." She went over to the one at the door who had ordered everyone to stay put. He was besieged by diners asking questions, but he was just repeating his instructions to go back to their tables and stay put. When he saw Melissa push her way to the front, he waved her forward. They spoke for a couple of minutes then she returned to the table. "Apparently Truong grabbed the gun of one deputy and used it to shoot them both then fled."

"Wasn't he in cuffs?"

"The court doesn't allow cuffs in the courtroom during trial if a defendant has been cooperative and has no record of violence, even in a murder case. It prejudices the jury, or so the argument goes. They took him out of the courtroom and were about to cuff him in the hallway when it happened. He fled through the courtroom still holding the gun. He headed down the stairway. They don't know where he is now."

"How are the deputies?"

"I don't know. The ambulances are just arriving. They may not be allowed to enter the courthouse until they can verify whether the shooter is still inside."

It was another forty minutes before everyone was allowed to leave. Ingram found out that they had reviewed the security tapes and found that Truong had escaped through an emergency exit immediately after getting to the ground floor. He was in civilian clothes for the same reason he wasn't cuffed. It prejudiced the jury to see someone in a jail jumpsuit. That meant he could blend right into the community.

"So what am I supposed to do?" Cliff asked. "I'm supposed to stay available until the trial is over."

"Yeah, I don't know. The judge is either going to postpone the trial or continue it without the defendant. A defendant waives his right to be present by fleeing. The trial can continue in absentia. Can you hang around until tomorrow at least? We should know by then."

"I guess I'll have to."

They said their goodbyes and Cliff returned to his hotel to extend his stay.

At five o'clock Ingram called Cliff and told him that the judge had decided to continue the trial without Truong. Cliff should stay available in case he had to testify the next day.

Transcript
THE COURT: Mr. Bollinger, call your first witness.

BOLLINGER: I call Detective Slonsky back to the stand.

THE COURT: Detective Slonsky, you've already been sworn. Your oath still applies. Please take the stand.

BOLLINGER: I have only one question, Detective. You've already testified that you arrested my client and gave the Miranda warnings and that he never said anything after that. My question is when you arrested him, did he make any statements before you Mirandized him?

End transcript.

Slonsky looked over to Ingram. Truong had claimed his innocence. Was this an underhanded way to get his denial of guilt in without putting him on the stand? Ingram rose to object and Slonsky held his tongue. Ingram paused for a few moments then sat back down without saying anything. The judge looked at her quizzically.

Transcript
THE COURT: Ms. Ingram? Anything?

INGRAM: No objection, your honor.

THE COURT: The witness may answer.

SLONSKY: I told him he was under arrest for murder. He said "I never murdered anyone."

BOLLINGER: No further questions.

INGRAM: No questions, your honor.

THE COURT: The witness is excused.

BOLLINGER: I move for a mistrial. My main witness is unavailable.

THE COURT: The jury will recess to the jury room. We have a legal matter to attend to.

[The jury leaves the courtroom]

THE COURT: Mr. Bollinger, what's the idea? Your 'main witness,' I take it, is the defendant.

BOLLINGER: Yes, your honor.

THE COURT: You argued this yesterday *in camera* after he escaped. You know my ruling. I'm not going to let the defendant's actions delay the administration of justice. He waived the right to be present by fleeing.

BOLLINGER: But the jury must know about the shooting. That's sure to prejudice them on this case.

INGRAM: Your honor, we went over this yesterday. The jury was already in the jury room when the defendant committed yet another murder in the secure hallway. We polled them last night and none of them were aware of the shooting. They were just told to remain in the jury room while a security matter was in progress. You sequestered them in a hotel overnight with instructions not to watch or read the news or talk to anyone. We polled them this morning and they all say they followed the court's instructions. All they know is that the defendant is not present. They don't know why. There's no prejudice.

THE COURT: I agree. Even if they were aware, it would be because of the defendant's actions. He cannot obtain a mistrial by prejudicing the jury against him with his own misdeeds. The motion is denied. Bring in the jury. [The jury is seated] Call your next witness, Mr. Bollinger.

BOLLINGER: I have no further witnesses, your honor. The defense rests.

THE COURT: Ms. Ingram, anything further?

INGRAM: Yes, your honor. I would like to recall Mr. Knowles. I have some additional physical evidence I would like to introduce through Mr. Knowles. It will take a couple of hours to arrange this.

BOLLINGER: I object. The state has rested their case in chief. They can't introduce new evidence at this point. They can only bring in rebuttal evidence. I didn't question Mr. Knowles.

INGRAM: It is rebuttal evidence. It pertains directly to Detective Slonsky's evidence a moment ago.

THE COURT: Has Mr. Bollinger been provided a copy of this evidence?

INGRAM: Yes, your honor. He's had it for at least three months.

THE COURT: I'll review the new evidence outside the jury's presence when we resume. The court is in recess until two p.m. The jury will remain sequestered.
[the court is in recess]

[the court is in session]
THE COURT: We're back on the record in the case of the State of Nevada versus Van Truong. I have reviewed the evidence in question. I'm prepared to hear arguments. Mr. Bollinger?

BOLLINGER: Your honor, there are so many things wrong with this recording I don't know where to begin. Mr. Bui was clearly under duress. Mr. Knowles was torturing him. It's hearsay. There was no Miranda warning. It's so highly prejudicial that I'd have to ask for a mistrial again if the jury heard this. It would be almost impossible for a jury to find my client not guilty. You ruled before trial that the state could not introduce evidence related to the death of Raven Tran for that reason.

INGRAM: Mr. Bollinger seems to know where to begin after all. As to hearsay, it's a dying declaration, a statement by a co-conspirator, and a statement against penal interest. There're three exceptions for you. Mr. Knowles was not torturing Mr. Bui. Mr. Bui may have been in agony, but it was only because he attacked Mr. Knowles and was shot in return. He brought it about himself. Mr. Knowles had no way to relieve him of that pain. Mr. Knowles doesn't carry morphine around with him in case he has to help someone who tries to kill him. Mr. Knowles is a private citizen, not a government agent, so Miranda doesn't apply. Even if it did, Mr. Truong doesn't have standing to assert Mr. Bui's constitutional rights. As for the last point, of course it is highly prejudicial, which is why the state had no problem abiding by the court's ruling earlier. We didn't try to introduce this tape in our case in chief. But Mr. Bollinger opened the door when he asked Detective Slonsky about the defendant's statement. He said he never murdered anyone. This recording is direct evidence that the defendant did murder someone and is thus a liar. He doesn't get to introduce a self-serving statement by the defendant without the state being able to cross the defendant or rebut that statement.

THE COURT: Enough. Ms. Ingram is correct on all points. You took a chance, Mr. Bollinger, and you lost. You've had that tape in your possession for months. You argued against its admission before trial and you won. You should have let well enough alone. I warned you that if you opened the door, the tape would be fair game. The recording will be admitted into evidence once Mr. Knowles authenticates it. Your objections are on the record. Don't repeat them in front of the jury during questioning. You can argue them during closing. You can appeal if you like. Bring in the jury.

End transcript.

The jury was brought in and the recording Cliff made on Bui's phone was played. Ingram then took Cliff through the whole story of the plane crash, his survival ordeal, and the gunfight with Bui. The jurors sat gaping and glaring at the defense table. Bollinger never objected once and didn't cross-examine Cliff.

The state rested and the defense put on no further witnesses. Closing arguments were brief since the tapes were so conclusive. The judge gave the jury its legal instructions and sent them in to deliberate. They came back in forty-five minutes with a guilty verdict. Murder in the first degree.

Afterward, Ingram, Slonsky, and Cliff adjourned to her office. Several of her colleagues gave her high fives. A few asked Cliff for his autograph or to take selfies with him. They settled in a conference room for some privacy.

"Great job all around. Thank you, gentlemen. You both did a terrific job on the stand."

"Just doing our job," Cliff replied.

"It's not your job, hotshot," Slonsky spit out. "You FBI guys are all the same. I worked this case for eight years and you come in at the last minute and take all the glory."

Cliff replied calmly. "I didn't ask to be here. I was subpoenaed. You're getting paid; I'm not. In fact, I'm losing money being here instead of working. I'm the one who got hunted and shot while you sat in your office doing paperwork. Where's Dice now, huh? From what I hear you haven't lifted a finger to find him."

"Alright, enough cockfighting," Ingram interrupted. "We should be celebrating, not arguing about who gets the credit."

"I'm retiring in three weeks. Your office is pursuing it now. There's a case out of San Jose for Tran's murder and one here in Vegas for the plane sabotage. The FBI sure likes to suck up the headlines."

Ingram's voice grew louder. "Knock it off, Detective. Cliff's not FBI anymore. You're the ones who requested a federal warrant originally on the Mendoza murder. Now Dice's wanted in San Jose and he'll be charged with the murder of the two court deputies later this week here, too. Your departments should be cooperating."

"I have a question, Melissa," Cliff said. "Can Dice appeal the verdict? I don't mean can he win. Can he appeal at all? He's not here. Does he have to sign something within a certain period of time?"

"The law is murky in that area. Usually if a defendant becomes a fugitive after conviction, but before appeal, he can still appeal, although that's not universally held. If he flees after the appeal has been filed, normally the appeal is dismissed."

"Why?"

"It doesn't matter. This case is unique. All the case law I know involves defendants who were convicted and appealed while still present and then refused to surrender, becoming a fugitive that way, not shooting someone mid-trial and fleeing. I've never seen a case where the flight occurs during trial and the conviction takes place while he's still a fugitive. But I don't think it'll matter. Bollinger may file an appeal, but he won't fight my motion to dismiss it and the court isn't going to hear the appeal."

"How do you know?" Slonsky said. "He has a constitutional right to appeal, doesn't he?"

"No. The right to appeal is purely statutory, not constitutional. The court can interpret the rules however they want. Dice killed two court personnel. Judges know that those deputies are the ones who protect them from angry defendants and civil litigants. There will be no breaks for Truong from the appellate panel. The appellate judges will find the appeal invalid if Bollinger misses a single comma, which I'm sure he will."

Cliff looked puzzled. "You said Bollinger wouldn't fight your motion to dismiss any appeal. That doesn't make sense. Why would he appeal and then not oppose a motion to dismiss?"

Ingram smiled knowingly. "You still don't get it, do you? Bollinger's just going through the motions. He's on our side now."

"Huh?" Slonsky grunted.

Cliff caught on immediately. He looked at Slonsky. "That was intentional, putting you on the stand and asking that question about Dice's statement he didn't kill anybody. He knew exactly what was going to happen. Right?" He turned to Ingram for confirmation.

"Cliff's right. Clyde's actually a decent guy. After the courthouse shooting there was no way he was going to help Truong, but he still had a duty to continue as his counsel. The court wouldn't let him withdraw. He made it look like he was trying to get that exculpatory statement Dice made into evidence, but he was really opening the door for me to introduce the Bui tape."

"Whatever. I'm outta here." Slonsky stood to leave.

"I'll be going, too," Cliff said. "Congrats on the conviction."

The men left and went their separate ways. Back at the hotel Cliff called Maeva. She was back in the Bay Area holding down the fort.

"How'd it go?" she asked. "Did they catch him?"

"No, he's still on the loose. The trial went fine. Convicted of murder in the first degree."

"So you're coming home today?"

"Actually, no. I'm thinking of staying for a little while."

"Why?"

"How's it looking there? Busy?"

"Not very. You cleared the calendar in anticipation of the trial."

"Why don't you join me."

"In Vegas? Doing what?"

"There's a certain fugitive who ordered a hit on me. I'd like to see him in custody."

"Whoa. You're going after Dice on your own? You're not serious."

"I am. And you know more about his operation here than almost anyone. You'd be a big help."

"Cliff, come home. Leave the commando stuff to the cops. You're no SWAT guy. Neither am I. Dice is a killer. You don't want to mess with him. I know I sure don't."

"I don't want to mess with him. I don't want to confront him or get anywhere near him. I just want to track him down. I don't have any confidence in the P.D. here. Slonsky's as sharp as a rubber ball. If you aren't game, I'll do it on my own. Come on, just for a couple of days."

Maeva let out a big sigh. "Okay, two days. That's all, and we don't go anywhere there's a chance he could be."

"He could be anywhere. That would rule out leaving my hotel room."

"You know what I mean. We stay away from anywhere we actually think he is."

"Deal. I'm going to get started by myself. I'll get you a room here. Take an early flight tomorrow and I'll pick you up. Bring a kit."

Chapter 22

Cliff went over in his head what he knew about Truong. He'd killed his brother-in-law Mickey Mendoza and his ex-girlfriend, Raven Tran. He'd run, and probably was still running, a gang that distributed drugs and fenced stolen goods. He probably used Duc Bui and Clyburn Airport as the import route. Cliff wanted to start with the airport, but felt it would be better to do that with Maeva, since she had gotten to know the personnel there. So what about Mendoza?

Why had Dice killed Mendoza? From what Slonsky had told him, the murder case was based almost entirely on identifying the getaway car as Tran's and on her taped confession. The forensics helped, but weren't conclusive. They'd never found a motive. Slonsky had just chalked it up to "that's what gangs do." Cliff knew that wasn't accurate. Mendoza was a member of Dice's gang according to Tran. Gang leaders don't kill their underlings the way television and movies sometimes portrayed them. Loyalty is a big thing. Gang killings are usually directed at rival gangs.

Prior to his testimony Cliff had reviewed the recording Tran had made. Unknown to Ingram, he'd recorded it on his own phone as he played it. That was a no-no, but not a crime. He really hadn't been paying all that much attention eight years ago when she'd made it. It had been Jim's case, not his, and it was all going to go to Las Vegas P.D. But listening to it again, he remembered how bitter Tran had sounded in talking about Dice in the car when she'd first been arrested. She'd called him a cheating bastard. She was smart enough not to talk in those terms on the recording. If she'd sounded like a spurned girlfriend, it would look like she was vengeful enough to lie about him.

So what did that have to do with Mendoza? Maybe nothing. It was worth looking into, though. He played back the part of her recording where she described arriving at Mendoza's house. She gave enough of a description that he could identify it. That was a starting point.

By the time he arrived at the location, it was late afternoon. The commute traffic had been horrible and his rented Tesla had a weak air conditioner. Cliff had changed into shorts and a T-shirt to look casual and he was glad of it. Tran had called it a house, but it was actually a duplex, one of two on the lot. They weren't side by side. One was near the street and the other, Mendoza's, was behind it, mostly concealed by the one in front. Between them was a paved area that doubled as car parking and a kids' play area. He parked across the street in front of a two-story stucco apartment building.

He realized he couldn't sit there long in the heat, idling to keep the air conditioning going, but he wanted to get the lay of the land. From Tran's description, he knew Mendoza's place was the back unit. As he considered his next move, he saw a UPS truck stop and drop off a package at the front unit. This gave him an idea. He watched for another minute to see if anyone opened the door and picked up that package. When no one did, he got out of his car, crossed the street and picked up the package.

He walked up the driveway holding the package. As he came to the paved area behind the front unit, he saw two children playing in an above-ground pool. A dark-haired boy of about nine standing in the water threw a golf ball across the pool and yelled "Go!." A blond girl a year or two older and a head taller had been standing across the pool with her back turned toward him. On his call she turned around and dove under the water. Ten or twelve seconds later she popped up with the golf ball in hand. She was about to throw it when she noticed Cliff.

"Do either of you kids know which unit is the Mendoza house? I have a package for them."

"I can take it," the boy said and started to get out of the pool.

"I'm sorry, I can only leave it at the address or with an adult."

The boy pointed to the door of the rear unit and rolled his eyes. Cliff could see now that he was probably a mix of Asian and Hispanic. He must be Mendoza's son with Dice's sister. He hadn't really expected Mendoza's widow to still be living in the same place eight years after his murder. He knew she was Dice's sister, but he didn't know her first or last name. Cliff took the package and started to set it down where the boy had pointed. Then he stood and declared in an exaggerated voice, "Oh, my mistake. This is for a Mr. Petrov." He started back around to the front.

As he disappeared around the corner of the unit he heard the girl say to the boy sotto voce, "What a moron. He can't even read." So much for respect for your elders.

He placed the package back where it had been on the step of the front unit and returned to his car. At least he knew where Truong's sister lived. This was spot number one where Truong might go for help. Cliff assumed she was likely to be willing to aid him. He was in no position to do a stationary surveillance, so he started the engine and was about to leave when he was startled by a knock on the rear passenger window.

A middle-aged woman wearing a floral blouse, polyester slacks, and Nikes was standing on the curb with her hand pressed to the window. He recognized the badge she was holding there. He used to carry one just like it. She slipped it back in her purse and he noticed the butt of a gun. She motioned for him to get out and follow her.

He turned off the engine, got out, locked the door, and walked around the car. "I'm Jean," the woman said as he approached. "In here." She led him into the apartment complex he'd parked in front of. They went into a hallway and up a flight of stairs. She took him to an apartment on the street side of the building and they went inside. "Grab a chair," she directed and waved toward the bedroom area. He picked up one of the cheap dinette chairs in the eating area and carried it into the bedroom where she led.

Sitting on the bed looking through a large telescope was a young male agent probably right out of the academy. Cliff knew the look. He'd been training agent for several just like him: muscular, a good shot, anxious for some action, not yet disillusioned by the humdrum existence of real FBI work. He looked Hispanic, with a thick head of black hair and a tattoo of the American flag on his forearm. The woman was white and nearing early retirement age. She must have been in the second or third wave of female agents the FBI recruited. The man kept peering through the telescope.

Jean extended her hand. "Cliff, I want to offer my congratulations. We all followed the case from when it hit the news. That was incredible how you not only survived the crash but took out Duck in the shootout. You're my hero. The whole office broke out in cheers when it was announced you'd been rescued."

Cliff assumed a sheepish grin and shook her hand. Before he could say anything in response, she continued, "Having said that, what the hell do you think you're doing? Are you even armed? What if Dice had walked out that door?"

"I wasn't going to knock. I just wanted to see the place where Mendoza was shot. I didn't know that Dice's sister still lived there."

"Well, she does. Bree Mendoza, and she's hostile. She could just as easily shoot you. Nevada's an open carry state. If you don't have a gun, you'd better get one or get out."

"So what's the FBI doing here? I thought the P.D. would be handling the local fugitive stuff. He hasn't fled the area that we know of yet. It has to be days before you can get a UFAP warrant."

"We aren't here on the UFAP, although I'm sure that'll be coming. It's a task force. We're FBI today; tonight LVPD comes in to take a shift. We have a major case going on the plane sabotage and obstruction of justice and witness tampering. That's you as victim. Victim, not investigator. Got it?" She pointed an accusatory finger at him.

"Yeah, yeah, I got it."

"Don't you answer your phone? The Bureau case agent has been trying to reach you. He went over to your hotel and you weren't there. His name's Barry Holder."

"I wondered who that was. I didn't recognize the number and I've been getting a lot of calls from reporters, so I didn't answer it. Several have tried to interview me at the hotel. I've been avoiding the area."

"He knows you were already interviewed in detail when you were back in the Bay Area, but the sabotage took place here. Of course your entire story is pretty much laid out in your court testimony. You don't want to go over that again. You'll just introduce minor inconsistencies. But there could be details about the plane or the crash you didn't cover."

"I'll answer his call next time. So the task force has this place staked out? Do you have street teams?"

"Of course. And a court order on her phone. We can only get texts, not voice, but it also gives us location. See the guy on the motorcycle kitty corner from us?" She pointed. "We have two other cars around the corner. Those are all FBI. We don't mix agencies on a shift because we have different radio channels for surveillance. He's wanted for the courtroom murders, too, although charges haven't been filed yet. The sheriff's office is part of the task force. Those were sheriff's deputies who died. If they're the ones to find him first, God won't be able to save him."

"Do you think he's still in the area?"

"Unlikely, but our best leads are here. Barry's over at Clyburn now. Dice may have flown out from there to avoid roadblocks or patrols on the highways and all the security at the commercial airport. Now that we know about Bui, we know Dice has pilots working with him. Look, we've got this covered. The best thing for you to do is just leave. Your face is too well known here now. You'll just burn our people and make everyone put up their defenses."

"All right. I won't go looking for him. I'm pleased to see you have such a big operation. I'll leave you to it."

"Glad to hear it. We'll keep you informed. Everyone knows you're still FBI family and the victim, too. You can find your way out?"

"Sure. Thanks, Jean. Nice meeting you. Good hunting."

Cliff left and headed back to the hotel. Maeva still wasn't here, so he didn't want to go to the airport yet. He decided to pick up a geocache or two while he had a free afternoon. At the hotel he pulled out his laptop, logged into the website and sorted by favorite points. The most favorited one was a virtual at the iconic Welcome to Las Vegas sign. There was also a traditional cache there. He put those on his list. He saw another virtual that was incredibly popular. It required going to the Stratosphere Tower. Cliff had never been afraid of heights, but after the crash, he didn't want to tempt fate. He left that one off his list.

He headed out geocaching in his rental car, driving around from spot to spot this time, rather than walking through a particular neighborhood. He wanted to hit the stars of the geocache kingdom. As he cruised along, a song came through the car's Bluetooth. He kept his mp3 collection on his phone.

It was a teenage wedding and the old folks wished them well. You could see that Pierre did truly love the mademoiselle.

Cliff thought this was almost laughably appropriate as he headed to the second most favorite geocache in the area: one at a drive-through wedding chapel. He'd almost skipped it when an idea had occurred to him. The whole notion was so cheesy, so Las Vegas, that it represented the worst of the city to him in a way; but sometimes bad taste has its virtues, too. The cache was popular for a reason. Love is universal and a very strong force. It can cause people to make rash decisions like getting married at a drive-through wedding chapel. Sometimes, as Chuck Berry tells us, that works out well. But not always. What if the motive for the Mendoza killing wasn't drugs, money or anything else gang-related. What if it was jealousy or passion? Was Mendoza cheating on Bree? Did Dice take revenge on him for that? Or maybe he beat or abused her and Dice was playing the big brother protector out of love for his sister?

He'd have to think about that. When he spoke to the FBI case agent, he'd mention these theories to him. Right now, it was geocaching time. He didn't get back until four hours later. He sat down to log his caches, the first long geocaching excursion he'd had in months, and he loved every minute of it.

Chapter 23

When Cliff picked up Maeva from the airport the next morning, she carried only one small bag. He knew her well enough to know that was her signal to him that she wasn't staying long, and, therefore, neither was he. He was old enough to be her father, but she was bound and determined to mother him.

"The plane landed forty minutes ago. What took you so long?" he asked as he pulled onto the highway.

"I had to check my bag. Baggage claim took awhile."

"That's small enough for carry-on."

She unzipped the bag and pulled out two semiautomatic pistols. The larger one she put in the console cup holder in its leather holster. "These had to be checked. That's yours. I'm strapping mine on now. I'm not letting you go Dice hunting unarmed. You can't conceal that. Remember, it's open carry here."

"Now you're being paranoid. I'm not going after him. I only want to dig up some leads. They've got a whole task force here. He's wanted on the Mendoza charge, the killing at the courthouse, the plane sabotage and ITAR-murder for Raven Tran. I'm sure they'll find him."

"You said you were going to get started on your own yesterday. What did you find out?"

"I went by the house where Mendoza was killed. His widow, Bree Truong Mendoza, still lives there. The task force spotted me and yanked me out of there. Apparently she's also a gang member. She's Dice's closest relative and confidante. She'd be the most likely to help him. But they've got her covered like a glove. I thought we'd go to the airport next. You know the people there. The FBI case agent was there yesterday. I missed him."

"Okay, but what's there? Dice won't be going anywhere near there."

"Not now, not with all the heat on, but I have a theory. He must know pilots, the ones who fly in the goods from L.A. or wherever. If I were him, I'd have hightailed it for Clyburn right from the courthouse and get one of my guys to fly me out. I don't think the deputies and P.D. would have thought to go there first. He could have gotten out that way."

"I think he would have been noticed. It was the middle of the day and he wouldn't have been a regular. Was he in a jail jumpsuit?"

"No, a nice business suit and tie. He'd have fit in."

"I know the airport manager. You want me to call him and arrange a meeting?"

"Good idea."

Maeva looked up the manager in her contacts and pressed the call icon. His secretary answered the phone.

"Hello. Is Mr. Pasquali there?"

"Miss Hanssen, I'm afraid he's too busy to take your call."

"I haven't even given you my name or told you why I'm calling."

"Your number is stored in our system. The phone displayed it. I'm afraid he's too busy."

"Too busy for me, you mean. Well, I don't think he's too busy to see my partner, Cliff Knowles. You know, the man your mechanic tried to murder. We're on our way there now. If the manager refuses to see him, I'm sure the reporters who I know are hanging around there will be interested in hearing that."

"Just a moment." Two minutes later Pasquali came on the phone.

"Miss Hanssen. How are you?"

"Fine, thank you. Did your secretary tell you we're on our way there now?"

"She mentioned that. Really, this is a terrible time for this. The FBI was here yesterday. The last time you were here it was the police. We don't know anything about this terrible event. We've cooperated with everybody."

"You haven't cooperated with Mr. Knowles yet. You're about to get your chance."

"I'm just leaving for a meeting. I'm afraid I won't be here. I'll have my assistant help Mr. Knowles. I must run. It's been nice talking to you. Goodbye." The call terminated. Maeva looked at Cliff and shrugged half-apologetically.

Cliff snorted. "I'm so glad I had you come to help."

"Very funny. Pasquali's a jerk. He's worried about liability. There are some other people there. The security staff is pretty helpful."

A few minutes later they pulled into the Clyburn parking lot. Maeva led him through the lobby where there were at least three reporters and a couple of television cameramen. One of the reporters recognized Cliff and ran up to him, mike in hand, but Cliff and Maeva disappeared into the manager's office anteroom before he could get his question out.

Pasquali's secretary was a bosomy woman of forty with smoker's skin and plucked eyebrows. She told them to have a seat and said someone would be right with them. Five minutes went by with no word from the woman or anyone else. Maeva noticed some employees walking past the office door and looking in. She spotted Robin Nguyen among them. She whispered to Cliff to stay there while she ran out for a minute. She caught up with Robin in the hallway.

"Robin. It's me, Maeva."

"Oh, hi. I'm so glad your partner is okay. It's all everyone's been talking about. Is that him?"

"Yes. What's going on? I thought you worked nights. Where's everybody going?"

"We all got called in for a special meeting. The lawyer for the owner is here. The meeting's starting in the hangar area. I think they're going to tell us not to say anything. We were warned that we were all going to be sued."

"This isn't about some lawsuit against the company. We don't care about that. It's about Dice … and your sister. Talk to Cliff now. They haven't told you not to yet."

"My sister? She died years ago."

"You don't follow the news? I guess you haven't heard. Just give us a few minutes." She took Robin by the elbow and led her back to the manager's office. From outside the anteroom door she motioned for Cliff to come out.

"What is it?" he asked, stepping into the hallway.

"I shouldn't be seen talking to you guys," Robin said. "Not here. Follow me." She led them back to the rental car booth, which was currently unmanned. There was a small office behind it where they could talk out of sight. Once safely out of sight, she put a hand on Cliff's arm and said, "I'm so glad you're safe. They're saying Doug wrecked your plane somehow and you almost died."

"Thank you. And you are…?"

"Robin Nguyen."

"Raven Tran's sister," Maeva added.

"Robin, we're trying to find out whatever we can to help the FBI find Dice. He's the one who sent Bui to kill me. He's also the one who killed Raven. I'm so sorry for your loss. I liked her."

"Wait! What? You knew my sister?"

"The pilot who died in the crash and I were FBI agents back then. We arrested her back in San Jose. She cooperated. She seemed honest to me. I did like her. After she was sent back here, she fled again and that's when Dice killed her."

"They told us she OD'ed. I knew she used drugs."

"She did OD, but that was because Dice spiked her heroin with fentanyl." Robin's mouth fell open in disbelief. Cliff pulled out his phone and started playing Bui's recorded statement.

"That prick!" She exclaimed when the recording ended. "She left him. He was a cheat. She didn't want anything more to do with him. He didn't need to kill her."

"You can help us. You know he's on the loose. He killed the deputies at the courthouse."

"I know. The police and FBI were all over this place yesterday. I talked to them, but I don't know anything. I have no idea where he is. I never even knew him, just what Raven would tell me about him. We kind of lost touch when she got in with that crowd, but she'd come home for family celebrations sometimes and confide in me."

"Maybe you know more than you think. I'm trying to figure out why Dice killed Mickey Mendoza. He was a loyal gang member, from what they tell me."

"I wouldn't know anything about that."

"I'm wondering if maybe it was personal. Maybe Mendoza abused Bree, Dice's sister. Maybe he was protecting her. Or maybe Mendoza was cheating on her and he went to teach him a lesson."

"I don't think so. Raven told me Dice used to bad-mouth his sister. He went out to clubs with Mickey. He liked Mickey better than Bree. Besides he cheated on Raven. It wouldn't bother him if Mickey cheated on Bree."

"Dice had another girlfriend? Do you know who it was?"

"Not for sure, but I think so. After Raven told me he was cheating on her, I saw him at the mall with this girl who was in my high school. They looked like, well, you know, they were together."

"What's the girl's name?"

"Jasmine. I don't know her last name. She was three years ahead of me."

"I'd like to talk to her. Do you know how I could find her? Do you know where she lives?"

"I don't know where she lives, but I know where she works. Or where she used to work, anyway. The Critter Care vet office. I took my mom's dog there once and she was behind the desk answering phones. That was a couple of years ago."

"What does she look like?" Maeva asked, interrupting. "As pretty as you?"

Robin blushed. "Oh, you silly. Maeva, you're the pretty one."

Cliff retook control. "Robin, I think what Maeva is fishing for is identifying information. We need to be able to recognize her. You know, race, hair and eye color, build."

"She's Vietnamese, like me. My size."

There was a knock on the office door. Someone outside yelled Robin's name and told her to get her ass to the all-employee meeting. After they heard the footsteps move away, Robin whispered that she had to go. She poked her head out and saw no one she recognized. She told Cliff and Maeva to wait a minute after she left before coming out. They thanked her for her help and watched her slip out quietly and disappear. After a minute they re-entered the lobby.

Cliff and Maeva returned to the manager's office. When they entered the anteroom, the secretary directed them into Pasquali's private area. A prim-looking Asian woman sat behind the desk. She wore a navy blue pantsuit with a cream blouse with ruffles. Matching gold earrings, bracelet and pendant completed her ensemble. Her makeup was heavy, but well-done, shaving a good five or ten years off her forty-five. She stood and greeted them coolly, identified herself as Lisa Mao, then motioned for them to be seated.

"Mr. Knowles, I want to extend my heartfelt condolences on the loss of your friend, Mr. Crosby, and on the hardships you've endured. It's a blessing and a testament to your resolve that you survived the ordeal."

"And who are you exactly? I thought a Mr. Pasquali was the manager here."

"He is. I'm counsel for the company. Here's my card." She handed him a business card embossed with the names of a law partnership.

"And what company is that?"

"Clyburn Aviation. The airport is a privately owned corporation. It was founded by the Clyburn family back in the fifties, but it's been expanded over the years and incorporated. It's run by a board of directors. They've sent me here."

"To do what, if I may ask? They're afraid I'm going to sue?"

"Any company would be derelict in its responsibilities if it did not seek to minimize litigation and the chance of liability. But I've been directed to cooperate fully. The company wants you to know that it had nothing to do with whatever Mr. Bui may have done to your plane or to you personally. He was not an employee. He rented space and performed services for the pilots or plane owners."

"I'm not here to threaten you with a lawsuit or make a claim for damages. I'm trying to help the police and FBI find Truong. He's the leader of the gang that sabotaged our plane, and I have reason to believe they use this airport to transport drugs and stolen goods."

"Mr. Knowles, the FBI was here all day yesterday and the police as well. We've cooperated fully with law enforcement and will continue to do so. We certainly hope the suspected murderer is apprehended."

"He's more than suspected. He *is* a murderer and this is his place of business. One of them."

"Now, hold on. That can be interpreted as a threat."

"Not a threat. A warning. He's dangerous, and he must have pilots coming in and out of here who work with him. I believe that you could identify them by examining flight records. He could show up and try to get flown out of here."

"Mr. Knowles, as you know, we can't reveal private information about our clients. Pilots are our customers. You're an attorney yourself, I understand."

"I know no such thing. There is no airport-client confidentiality. You may be a lawyer, but the company isn't. It could turn over its records to the police or FBI. The sooner he's caught, the safer your employees will be. If you're worried about liability, think about what it would cost if he shows up here and law enforcement has a shootout or barricaded hostage situation on its hands."

"As I said, we're cooperating fully. The safety of our employees and the public is our highest priority. We'll comply with all proper legal process."

"In other words, you're not volunteering anything."

"We know nothing about Mr. Truong's whereabouts, nor about any illegal activity that may have occurred, or may be occurring, at our facility. I don't see how I can help you. We respect your position and what you've been through, but you aren't law enforcement and there's nothing we can really share with you."

"What happens in Vegas stays in Vegas. That's what you're saying, isn't it?" Maeva chimed in.

"Miss Hanssen, the last I've heard, private investigators don't have any legal client confidentiality protection either, but you don't share your clients' personal details with anyone without legal process, especially not with people trying to find them guilty of something, now do you?"

"Our clients aren't running a drug and fencing ring with our help."

"No? Perhaps not, but if I'm not misinformed, you've represented an accused murderer."

"Accused, yes, but falsely accused." Maeva was leaning forward, looking like a panther ready to pounce.

"And our clients and employees are being falsely accused here, so far as we know." Mao remained calm and unintimidated.

Cliff put his hand on Maeva's shoulder and stood. "Alright, enough. This is pointless. Let's go."

Back out in the lobby a male reporter spotted Cliff and sidled up to him. He asked Cliff what he learned from "the car rental girl." This sent a jolt of concern through Cliff. The reporter had seen him talking to Robin. Who else had noticed? Had he put Robin in danger? He didn't know, but he vowed to be more careful from then on. He told the reporter that he was just discussing car rental, but it was clear the reporter didn't believe him. The man trailed them both out to Cliff's car but got nothing more from them.

Chapter 24

"So what else do we have?" Cliff asked in the car.

"I still have a list of the airport employees. They'll probably all be told not to talk to us, but maybe some are home today and not at the meeting. We could check out Jasmine, I suppose, if we can find her."

"If she and Dice are still hooking up he could be staying with her. I don't want to show up there. We can give the task force that lead."

"Do you think they know about her?" Maeva asked.

"I don't know. Let's go around your list of employees for now."

Maeva pulled up her list and began reading off names. Unfortunately, the list did not include home addresses, or other contact info. After some discussion, they decided to head to the hotel. Maeva still had to check in and they wanted to do some research on the employees with their laptops.

It was too early for Maeva to check in so they went to Cliff's room and fired up their computers. They split up the list and began doing Google, Facebook and other media searches on the names. Maeva got the first hit.

"Okay, this guy is good. Riley. He's a security guard. He was cooperative. He talked to me and took me seriously when I was here before. But I saw him go into the all-employee meeting this morning. We won't be able to talk to him until later." She turned her computer toward Cliff so he could see.

"Who's that with him?" Cliff was looking at a picture on Riley's Facebook page where a powerfully-built black woman was standing next to him, both wearing uniform polo shirts with the security company logo.

Maeva turned it back and read the comments. The picture showed a happy birthday sign in the background. Several comments wished him a happy birthday or made teasing remarks about him being over the hill. Three of the names of the commenters were women's names. Maeva looked at the list. Only one appeared on the list, a Laura Jackson. "I remember he told me his boss was a woman. That's probably her. She was going to isolate the tarmac security video for the period when your plane was there at Clyburn."

Cliff logged into the paid service he used for finding contact information on people, a necessity for any private investigator. He entered Jackson's name and the state of Nevada into the search fields. This brought up three women with that name in the Las Vegas area. It took only two minutes to narrow it down to the woman on Riley's page. She lived right in the city, not far from Clyburn.

"I don't remember seeing her at the airport," Cliff said. "There weren't any black women that I remember when we went through and she's pretty distinctive. She's taller than Riley. How tall was he?"

"He was a big guy. Over six feet. She must be massive."

"She may no longer be there. Let's give her a try. I have a phone number for her from the database." He dialed the number. It rang several times and then a voice answered, but it wasn't Jackson's. It was an automated voice telling the caller that the recipient was using the Google Assistant to screen calls and to go ahead and state his business. Cliff stated his name and began to leave a voice message when Jackson broke into the call.

"Mr. Knowles, I'm so glad you're safe. I worried about you for days."

"So you know who I am?"

"Of course. You're all over Instagram and Twitter. The Tik Tok of you coming out of the helicopter in California has over three million views. Your assistant was like a bulldog when she was here before asking about you and the plane. I didn't meet her, but she intimidated my guard. I was wondering if I'd ever see you."

"She's my partner, not my assistant, and she is persistent. We're here in Las Vegas and we'd like to talk to you. Are you free?"

"I'm at another location now. I can spare the time but I can't leave. I'll text you the address. Did you want to come now?"

"Yes, if you can." She agreed and they hung up. A few seconds later the address came through on a text. "Let's go." He started to strap on his gun and holster, but decided not to. This was not a hostile interview and many places did not allow guns inside, even though the state may be open carry. It was still legal despite signs to the contrary, but if asked to leave because of the gun, it was trespassing not to leave.

They headed to the business section of town. They found the address to be a large high-rise populated by finance firms, commercial real estate, and legal offices. Just off the lobby was a day care center. They asked the guard manning the reception desk for Laura Jackson. He directed them down a hallway and told them to knock on the door marked Security.

Jackson asked them in and apologized for the spare furnishings. There was only one visitor chair for the two of them. Building security supervisors don't get plush digs. Maeva volunteered to stand.

Cliff took in Jackson's full height, which stretched into six foot six plus territory. He wasn't good at judging heights over that. If he had to crane his neck to make eye contact, that classified as tall. She wore the same company uniform shirt she'd worn in the photo on Riley's Facebook page. Her name tag held her name and the title Security Manager. She had a milk chocolate complexion and had her hair pulled back into a tight bun. Her arms showed evidence of years in the weight room.

Cliff looked around and saw a Lady Rebels poster on the wall. Jackson was featured along with her teammates sporting UNLV basketball uniforms. She noticed him noticing it and offered, "Yes, I played basketball. It's nice to meet you, Mr. Knowles. And you must be Miss Hanssen." She offered her hand to Maeva first. After perfunctory handshakes all around, she asked, "How can I help you?"

"Well, I guess you know the general story," Cliff answered. "I flew out of Clyburn with Mr. Crosby and the plane crashed. The official cause is sabotage. I believe it was Duc Bui who did it. I also think he was directed to do it by Van Truong, aka Dice, who is now a fugitive after killing two deputies at the courthouse yesterday. I'm hoping you can give me information to help locate Truong. I believe he was running drugs and stolen goods through that airport while you were security head there. I thought you might have suspicions about who those pilots were. Truong might have hitched a ride out of town from one of them."

"Why are you trying to locate Truong if he tried to kill you? As one security professional to another, my advice would be to get the hell as far away from here as you can."

"I don't want to actually find him myself; I just want to get some leads to give the FBI and police."

"I've already been interviewed by the NTSB, the FBI, and Las Vegas P.D. They have everything I know."

"Would you be willing to share that information with us?"

"I'd rather not. I found the whole business to be very disturbing and I want to stay out of it. That's why I asked for a transfer from Clyburn. I agree with you that there's something fishy going on there. The manager told me to destroy the security footage for the period when your plane was there. I told him I couldn't do that because it could be destruction of evidence. He threatened to fire me. Technically, I work for the security company, and that would just mean transferring to another client, but it would mean a drop in pay until I found an equivalent position. So I requested a transfer on my own."

"What did you do with the security footage?"

"I preserved a copy and gave it to the NTSB. I admit I was curious and took a look at it. It showed a figure late at night going out to Crosby's plane and doing something up on the top. That's where the fuel tanks are. Whoever it was turned off the lights on that side of the building, so they knew what they were doing. There's always some light at night from all the neon around here, so it was still possible to see his silhouette, but it was just a blurry shape. He wasn't recognizable. I'm pretty sure it was Bui, if that's what you want to know."

"What about the pilots? Who do you think might have been the ones helping with the drugs and goods?"

"I don't know. I told the FBI to get a list of Bui's regular customers. I don't have that. There were a couple of planes I know by sight that I know he serviced a lot. I told the FBI how to identify them from the fuel records. Don't ask me to tell you more about them. I don't know them and they may be totally innocent. I'm not going to get someone in trouble and I don't want to be sued for defamation. I gave it all to the FBI and police."

"You're a security professional, as you said. It's your job to protect your clients and their customers and cooperate with them when they have been victimized. I was one of those coming through that airport."

"I know that, and I'm sincerely glad you survived what must have been an awful ordeal. I'm sorry we didn't prevent that, but we aren't trained for that sort of thing or even intended to prevent it. And, first off, I am protecting you. Just go home; I'm giving you advice that could save your life. Second, I really don't know anything of value. I'm not an investigator. I just schedule guards and manage the cameras and door access cards. I'm just filling in my time until I complete my teaching credential. I want to coach high school basketball. I already have an offer but I need the credential."

Maeva tapped Cliff on the shoulder. "Cliff, I agree with her. We're running out of leads and the authorities seem to have all they need to do a thorough job. They've got more than we do, anyway. We really should get home and get out of their way. We have paying clients, in case you forgot." She smiled at Jackson to show her support.

Cliff didn't give up. As Maeva later described it, he tried a charm offensive on Jackson, but he was more offensive than charming. She was not forthcoming with any more information, so he finally gave up and headed out the door with Maeva right behind.

"Are we done yet?" She asked.

"We still have Jasmine to follow up on."

"I thought you didn't want to show up there. Dice could be at her place."

"I'm not going to go to her residence. I thought we'd just go by her employment."

"The vet's office? We don't know if she still works there. Did you find her last name? You can use the database."

"No, but we can always ask for her. If she doesn't work there we can try to find out where she is. Dice isn't going to be hanging out there. It's a public place of business."

"Fine," she sighed.

Cliff drove them to the vet's office. There was a spacious parking lot with plenty of empty slots. If this had been California, there would have been no more than two or three. Land costs a lot less in Nevada.

They stepped out of the car into the midday sun. The temperature was climbing, but it wasn't oppressively hot. Cliff started to head for the door when Maeva called to him. She was discreetly looking at the other cars in the lot. She waved him over.

"They may be able to see us from the windows. Don't look like you're snooping. Look over my shoulder at the silver Kia."

Cliff did as she suggested, gesticulating so that anyone seeing them from the building would think he was involved in an animated conversation. He glanced at the car and at first didn't see what had caught Maeva's attention. Then he spotted it: the personalized license plate JAZMIN3. It was in the row of cars closer to the street. There was another row of parking slots close to the building, with a wide driving lane separating them. He nodded and led her by the arm back to his car.

"Okay, here's what we'll do," he said, back in the car. "You go inside and take a quick look. If you see a Vietnamese woman like Robin described and you can tell that no one is looking out the window, text me and I'll plant a tracker. If it's not clear, then try to distract them. You can act hysterical and tell them your neighbor said she found your cat injured and brought him here or whatever. When they're all busy dealing with you, text me and I'll do it then." Cliff opened up the kit he had asked Maeva to bring and pulled out a tracking device.

"I don't know. That sounds too complicated and they'd have my face. They probably have security cameras. Let's do it like we did that Chrysler last year. Let me drive."

They switched places and Maeva drove out of the parking lot. She pulled over into a strip mall parking lot two blocks away and parked for twenty minutes. When she felt any memory of their brief lull in the lot had been forgotten by anyone who may have noticed, she headed back to the vet's parking lot. She approached slowly, checking to be sure no one was in the lot. As it turned out, a customer was parking near the Kia, so Maeva drove on by. She circled the block once and came back around. This time it was clear. As they pulled close, Cliff ducked down out of sight.

Maeva pulled into the lot and rolled along until her car was right behind the Kia, blocking the view from the building. Cliff was on the street side. She whispered "Go." Cliff eased open the passenger side door and slipped out quickly without raising his head above window level. He closed the door quickly and quietly. Meanwhile, Maeva lifted up her travel bag, which was still in the car, and positioned it on the steering wheel, then began rummaging through it like she was looking for something. If anyone in the building was watching them, they would be likely to focus on her activity and the open bag also blocked most of the view through the car windows, so that it would be hard to see the passenger door on the far side open.

Cliff got down on his knees and looked under the Kia. He placed the tracker and reversed the process, getting back into the car, still staying below window level. Maeva put away her bag and drove out of the lot. Cliff wished they'd had tracker technology back when he'd been in the FBI. He'd spent countless hours sitting in a car on surveillance.

They went to the hotel and got Maeva checked in. Then it was lunchtime. As they were eating in the hotel restaurant, a reporter came up to Cliff and asked him to do an interview. Cliff told him to leave him alone and let him eat his lunch. The reporter ignored the request and kept peppering him with questions. At one point he asked Cliff if he was afraid Truong would come gunning for him.

"What? Are you serious? Why would he come after me? The trial is over. He's been convicted. He's going to be sentenced in absentia. I have nothing to do with any of that now. Killing me wouldn't help him."

"I've heard rumors he's out for revenge."

"Rumors from whom?"

"Law enforcement sources."

"How would they know his intentions? They don't know where he is or what he's doing."

"Maybe they have sources in the gang."

"That's bull. Leave me alone. I'd like to finish my lunch."

The reporter tried a few more times, but gave up when neither Cliff nor Maeva rose to the bait. They finished their lunch in peace. As they were having coffee and discussing the case, something struck Cliff as not quite right.

"That reporter was lying," he said.

"About what?"

"Where he heard the rumor. If the police or FBI was in communication with a gang member in touch with Dice, they'd have been able to track him down and arrest him. They certainly would have warned me of any information he was gunning for me. There's only one person I know of who would be likely to know that – Bollinger."

"Ingram says he's on our side now. Maybe we should go talk to him."

"We will."

Cliff searched for Bollinger's number online and dialed it. He reached a secretary and said he'd like to meet with Bollinger today. She asked him for his name, which he gave. She put him on hold for several minutes. When she came back on, she told him Mr. Bollinger was not available. Cliff asked when he could get an appointment and she replied that he had no appointments available in the foreseeable future. Cliff didn't bother to argue. He hung up.

"He's avoiding me, but he's there."

"So, do you want to drive or shall I?"

"My turn."

Thirty minutes later they were on 6th Street in front of a three-story faux classical stone monstrosity braced by Doric pillars and two palm trees. The sign outside read "Essex Manor Law Offices." They climbed the grandiose marble steps and entered the lobby. More marble stonework greeted them there. A receptionist sat at a desk. Behind him was a listing of the building tenants. There were at least four law offices, all appearing to be solo practitioners. The receptionist asked who they were there to see. Cliff said Clyde Bollinger. The receptionist directed him to the third floor. They went on up.

The elevator opened onto the lobby of Bollinger's office. There was no other tenant on that floor. From the size of the office Bollinger must have had at least two other attorneys and several paralegals working for him, probably more. On a padded chair to their right sat a swarthy, heavily tattooed man wearing jeans and a T-shirt and fiddling with his phone. Cliff and Maeva both pegged him as a likely client. A young woman appearing to be of Middle Eastern descent sat at the reception desk and asked if she could help them.

"I'm Cliff Knowles. I'm here to see Clyde Bollinger."

The woman was alarmed, but regained her composure enough to blurt out, "I told you he wasn't available." She wasn't composed enough to keep from glancing down the right-hand hallway with a worried expression.

Cliff led the way down the hallway in fast strides, Maeva right behind. The receptionist scrambled to get ahead of them but her painful-looking strappy heels made that a non-starter. She yelled out from behind them, "Mr. Bollinger, I tried to stop them."

At the end of the hall was a large office with Bollinger's name on the nameplate. As they entered, he was standing up with a putter in his hand trying to sink a golf ball into a plastic replica of a golf hole across the carpeted floor. He looked up.

"Really, Mr. Knowles. You know you can't do that," he said calmly, and putted the ball. It missed.

"I can see you're busy," Cliff replied deadpan. "This won't take long. Is Truong out on a mission of revenge? Are my family and I in danger?"

"You know I can't reveal confidential attorney-client communications."

"I know that any expression of intent to commit future crimes is not covered by attorney-client protection."

"I have to worry about my own family, too."

"So you're saying better for him to go after me than go after you for spilling the beans."

"It sounds to me like you've already been warned."

"Not by you. Is there any truth in it?"

"By a reporter, then?"

Maeva had listened to the whole colloquy and at this point the realization struck. She blurted out, "It was you! You tipped off the reporter and told him to let Cliff know. That was your way of giving the warning without it being traced back to you."

Bollinger smiled at her and gave an appreciative nod. "I'm no longer Truong's attorney, but I'm still ethically obligated to keep his past communications in confidence. So I cannot confirm or deny that."

Cliff looked at Maeva and gave her a small nod of approval. "Okay, we've got that out of the way. So where is Dice now?"

"I don't know. If I did, I would tell the authorities."

"You must have some idea. If you won't answer that, let me change the subject. Did he have a girlfriend eight years ago when Mendoza was killed?"

Bollinger looked at him quizzically, but said nothing.

"I'll ask it another way. Did Dice kill Mendoza because Mendoza was sleeping with Jasmine? That was it, wasn't it? A classic love triangle. Or maybe a quadrangle. Mendoza was cheating on Bree with Jasmine, the same girl Dice was cheating on Raven with. That was the motive for the murder."

Bollinger broke into a grin. "I have to hand it to you, Mr. Knowles. The police never figured that out. They thought it was gang business."

"Is he still seeing her?"

"I don't keep tabs on my clients' love lives. I already told you I don't know where he is. Now I really can't help you. I insist that you leave." He looked at the doorway behind Cliff. There was a security guard there filming the scene with her phone. She stepped forward and took Cliff's elbow.

This was actually a clever move, Cliff thought. If it had been the young man at the lobby reception desk, an athletic one hundred eighty-pounder, Cliff might have shrugged him off. But this guard was a fifty-five-year-old woman weighing maybe one hundred ten tops. He could hardly overpower her without looking like a brute.

"Fine. We're going." He gently lifted her hand off his arm and turned toward the door. Maeva followed him out of the office, the guard behind them both.

When they were back outside in the car, Maeva asked him, "How did you come up with that? Mendoza and Jasmine."

"Well, it was only a guess, of course, but it made sense. Yesterday while I was geocaching, I went through this drive-through wedding chapel. It got me to thinking how people do the craziest, most spontaneous things when they're in love. That may be a drive-through wedding, or something darker, like killing in a fit of jealousy. When Robin told us about Dice and Jasmine, I put it together. Mendoza was probably too smart to make a move on Raven, the boss's girl. She was off limits. She probably had no interest in him, anyway. Robin didn't mention anything like that. But Jasmine was apparently fair game. If he viewed her as a sideline, a gang fun-time girl, not together with anyone, he might have moved on her. He may not even have known she was already Dice's side squeeze."

"So it's confirmed. Bollinger didn't say so outright, but you obviously nailed it. That means that Jasmine was his girlfriend then and may still be."

"Right, and Bollinger says the police don't know that. The FBI probably doesn't, either."

"We need to let them know."

"First, I need to let Ellen know that Dice may be on a revenge mission. He apparently researched both me and Crosby long ago. He may very well have my home address."

Cliff dialed Ellen. She picked up on the third ring. He explained the situation. She told him that the San Francisco SAC had already put a security detail on their home address until Truong was in custody, but she would let him know that now the threat was real. They might beef it up. She also let him know in no uncertain terms that it was time to get his ass home. He had no business chasing around Las Vegas like he was still an agent. His family needed him all the more now. He agreed and promised he'd catch a flight home that night.

"Sounds like you finally got some sense drilled into you," Maeva said when the conversation was over. "I'll make the flight arrangements."

Cliff nodded and pulled out his own phone. While Maeva was making plane reservations, he was checking the tracker app on his phone. The tracker they'd placed on Jasmine's came with an app that Cliff and Maeva had both installed on their phones. The transmitter on the car determined its location in two different ways: GPS and wi-fi. The latter was more useful most of the time in urban environments. As the car moved around, the device detected nearby wi-fi signals. It wasn't necessary for the device to log on; they could identify the wi-fi just by its public signal. Services like Google provided a complete map of the United States and many other places identifying the location of every wi-fi signal its cars detected during the Google Maps Street View cruises. These locations were stored and every so often transmitted via the cell phone network to a central server which could be accessed through the app. It was also possible to send a request to the device for its current location and get a response.

The app showed that the car was in the veterinarian's office. But as he watched, the app showed the car start to move. While Maeva was on hold he showed her the app screen. She shrugged and said "So?"

"So, it's 2:30 in the afternoon. The vet's office is open till 5:00. What's her car doing leaving the lot?"

"I don't know. Maybe her shift is over. Maybe she went home early. What difference does it make?" The airline ticket agent came on the line at that point and Maeva returned to making flight arrangements.

Cliff sensed something wrong. He looked up the number of the vet's office and dialed it. It rang five times and was answered by an automated system assuring him that his call was important to them and his estimated waiting time was three minutes.

Five minutes later a female voice answered, "Critter Care."

"Hi. I'd like to speak to Jasmine."

"Speaking."

"Uh, I was just in your parking lot a little while ago and I saw someone drive your car away. At least I think it was yours. It had your name on the license plate. I had just seen you in the office there a few minutes before, so I knew it wasn't you driving it. I thought someone was stealing it, so I decided to call you."

"Oh. That's no problem. That was my boyfriend. He borrowed my car. He has a key. Thanks for letting me know. I have another call. I have to go."

Chapter 25

Maeva clicked off her phone. "Okay, we have a flight out for San Jose at seven fifteen. With slowdowns, we should be there two hours early. We can grab something to eat at the airport.

"Okay, sounds good."

"I'm glad you've come to your senses. Going after Dice just made no sense. The task force will round him up soon enough."

"Well, you're not the one he tried to have murdered."

"No, I'm not. Which is all the more reason why you should be the one most wanting to get out of here. You know how serious he is. Or was. I don't entirely buy the theory he wants revenge on you. He's got plenty of people responsible for his conviction. If I were in his shoes and wanted to go after someone, it would be the D.A. or the judge or even the jurors."

"Mm."

They rode along in the afternoon traffic for a mile or so with no conversation. Maeva spoke first. "You're awfully quiet."

"What's there to say?"

"Hold it. You missed the on ramp."

"I know a short cut."

"A short cut? The freeway goes right by the hotel. What's going on? You're being weird."

"I have something I have to do."

"Don't tell me – a geocache, right?"

"You guessed it."

"You and your geocaching. Okay, what's the name of it? I'll look it up and read the description. I can help you look for it."

"No need. I know where it is."

Maeva looked over at the phone in Cliff's hand. "Hey! That's not the geocaching app. That's the tracker. You're going after Jasmine. Why bother? She's probably just going home. You can wait until … hold on. I'm getting a bad feeling. You called her while I was on the phone with the airline, didn't you?"

"Yep."

"And?"

"She's still at the vet's office. She said her boyfriend was driving the car."

"Oh, hell, no. If that's Dice you want to be going the opposite direction. Take us back to the hotel. Come on, Cliff."

"It's probably not Dice. She was his side squeeze eight years ago. We don't know he's her boyfriend now. She's probably had five others since then. She was sleeping with Mendoza. I just want to drive by and make an ID before he gets out of the car, whoever it is. If it's Dice, I'll hightail it out of there. Don't worry, even if it's him, this Tesla can outrun that Kia."

"Dammit, Cliff, this isn't funny. Or responsible." She unhooked her seatbelt and strapped on her sidearm again. Even as she tried to talk Cliff out of his course of action, she knew he wouldn't be deterred. The seatbelt warning alarm sounded and flashed red on the dash.

"You aren't going to need that. Put your seatbelt back on. The only danger you'll face is going through the windshield if I have to stop suddenly."

Maeva buckled up again. "Okay, you keep your eyes on the road. I'll tell you where he's going. He's heading east. … Okay, now he's getting on 604 going toward Nellis Air Force Base. Hang a left at the Sam's Club. You can get ahead of him."

Cliff made the left turn and ran a light just after it turned from yellow to red. There was a screech of tires behind him. He didn't look back.

Maeva continued to navigate. "Keep going, then when you get to Las Vegas Boulevard, make a left. If he keeps going that way, he'll come up behind you pretty quickly. He's in the left lane, so you'll have to make the ID on your side. Once you're on Las Vegas Boulevard, stay in the right lane and I'll let you know when he's coming up on your left. You should be able to tell if it's him."

Cliff drummed his thumbs on the steering wheel nervously every time they got stopped at a stoplight, but the Kia was stopping at lights, too. It wasn't clear whether Cliff would end up ahead or behind.

"Left here. Good, we're ahead of him. Get in the right lane."

Cliff moved right.

"Okay, he should be coming up on your left in a minute. Go slow." Maeva twisted around to look out the Tesla's rear window. "I can see his car back there. He's the third car back. Second car. Next car."

The Kia passed them on the left, accelerating. Cliff craned his neck to see the driver. "Dammit! I'm not sure. It was a male. The glare on the window. I'm going to try to pull up next to him at the next light."

"Is that such a good idea? What if he recognizes you? You won't be able to pull away or back up."

But her objection was too late. The Kia stopped at the next stoplight and Cliff pulled up right next to it. Once again he craned his neck, but this time he was able to face the Kia and lower his head to see inside better. He straightened up and turned to face Maeva. Whispering, he said, "That's him! That's definitely Dice."

"Why are you whispering?"

"Oh. No reason, I guess. It just seemed … never mind."

"Okay, so that's Dice. Time to notify the task force and get out of town. Make a U at the next light and head back to the hotel."

The light turned green and the line of cars began moving. Dice never looked over to his right. Cliff let the Kia pull ahead and stayed behind and to the right, in its blind spot. Suddenly the KIA pulled into a small left turn only lane and made a turn into a side street.

Cliff rebuffed Maeva's suggestion. "I'm staying out of his sight. He just turned off. What's the name of that street?"

"Lamont."

"We'll give him some time to settle. Now that we know it's him, we don't need to get close. I'll pull up ahead and wait to see if he stops somewhere. Once he's inside somewhere, I'll go by just to get the address for the task force."

"Cliff, if you give them the car description and the neighborhood, that's all they need. Don't go poking around there. If he spots us …"

"What is it with you? I'm being careful. You've never been so cautious before. We got the tracker app and I want the tracker back, too. Those things are expensive. When the car stops, we'll wait. It's almost a hundred degrees outside. He's going to go inside somewhere. He's not going to see us. So what if he sees a Tesla drive by? There are plenty of them."

"He's turned off Lamont and now he's making another turn."

"Okay, I'm pulling over at this plasma place. We'll just wait. That looked like a residential area. He's probably got a hideout there somewhere. See? Perfectly safe."

"Fine. I'll tell you when it stops." She grabbed Cliff's phone and turned it so he couldn't see. He rolled his eyes, but didn't object.

Thirty seconds later the tracker app showed the Kia had stopped on a short residential street. Maeva read the address out loud and insisted they wait another five minutes to be sure he was in for good, then turned the phone to let him see where it was. He pulled out onto the road and at the next light made a U-turn. When he got to Lamont he turned and followed the path the Kia had taken as Maeva called out the rights and lefts. It was a residential area with narrow streets and modest desert-style one-story houses. As they got to the block where the Kia was parked, an unmarked Chevy Malibu blocked the roadway a few houses before. Two people were sitting in the car with the engine running. Out stepped a middle-aged woman and approached the Tesla.

"We meet again," she said, knocking on Cliff's window. It was Jean, the FBI agent who had taken him in to the lookout site at the Mendoza house.

"Jean. What's going on?"

"We're arresting Truong. That's him being hauled out now." Cliff could see in the front yard a few houses down the road three FBI agents wearing raid jackets and bullet-proof vests perp-walking a handcuffed Dice out into the yard. One of the agents began a thorough pat down.

"Man, that's a coincidence. We just figured out where he was. I was going there to get the address so I could give it to you. How did you find this location?"

Jean just smiled and said, "The case agent is here. He wants to talk to you. Go ahead and pull around. I'll move the car to let you by."

Cliff drove around the Chevy and pulled up to the curb in front of the house where the Kia was parked. A fortyish studly-looking FBI agent right out of central casting noticed the Tesla and came walking up to it. He smiled and flipped his creds for Cliff and Maeva to see.

"Hi. Can I get in with you? It's hot out here," he said. Cliff pushed the door unlock button and the agent climbed in the back seat. "Hello, Cliff. I'm Barry Holder. You're almost as hard to track down as Truong. You still haven't answered my calls or texts."

"Yeah, well, I've been busy. It looks like you got him. Good work."

"Thanks to you."

"Me? I didn't have anything to do with it. You were here when I drove up. I just figured it out."

"You had everything to do with it."

"What are you talking about?"

Holder looked at Maeva who gave him a sly smile. "Maeva, would you mind switching seats with me?" Barry and Maeva switched places. Once in the front seat, Holder reached down under the dash and pulled out an electronic device.

"Now wait a minute. Is that a tracker?" Cliff blustered. "You can't …"

"No, this is the live transmitter. The tracker is under the rear bumper."

"Transmitter?! You've been listening to us the whole time? You need a court order."

"Not with permission of one party to the conversation. You should know that. You were a legal advisor. You used to teach this stuff to agents."

"But I never gave permission."

Barry turned to look at Maeva and the proverbial light bulb went on over Cliff's head. He twisted to look back at Maeva who was grinning wide enough to split her face in two. She raised one finger then turned it to point at herself.

"Maeva! You gave permission? Wait a minute. There were times you weren't in the car. I might have been talking on the phone or …"

Barry replied calmly, "We got permission from your wife, too. She's on the same credit card you used to rent it. So technically she's co-lessee and can give permission. Besides, you aren't going to sue us. We just saved your ass. You'd have gone in there gangbusters."

"Not true. I was going to notify you … well, maybe if I'd seen him outside and he didn't look armed."

"'Didn't look armed.' Listen to you. For a smart guy you can say some pretty dumb things sometimes."

"Okay, maybe I was kind of … unreasonably motivated … with this one. He tried to murder me."

"Fortunately for you, you have two women who love you and who would prefer you not be shipped home looking like Swiss cheese."

“But why did you put a tracker and transmitter on my car? I didn’t have any inside info. You have a whole task force here who’s been following Dice’s gang for years. You were set up on Bree’s place. That was smart. You had no reason to think I’d be of any help.”

“Isn’t it obvious? We’re here. You led us right to him.”

“But that was luck. I mean, you couldn’t know I’d be able to find him. I didn’t know that.”

“It wasn’t luck. It was damn fine detective work. Look, Cliff, you don’t mind if I call you that do you? I feel like we’re old friends already, even though I’ve never met you before. I knew who you were since before you first arrived in Vegas. You’re something of a legend in the Bureau, whether you appreciate it or not. When I got assigned to this sabotage case, I talked to some agents in San Francisco Division who used to work with you. They said you were the best investigator they ever knew, which comports with your reputation. I knew you’d have some good ideas on how to catch him. But you kept ducking my calls. It was obvious you wanted to go after Dice on your own without me as your nanny.”

“I was going to return your calls.”

“‘I was going to return your calls’,” Barry echoed in a mocking voice. “After you’d caught Dice, maybe. So anyway, after Jean saw you out at the Mendoza place putting yourself and the whole task force at risk, I knew we had to do something about you. I called your wife and asked her if she’d help us get you out of Vegas. She didn’t think she could; she knows you. She’s the one who suggested wiring the car. She also called Maeva and asked her to go along with us. After that, it was just sit on you a few blocks away and listen to the genius at work. Thanks for the five minutes and the address, Maeva. That’s all we needed.”

“I never saw you. I’m good at spotting a tail.” Cliff said it with a note of pride.

“We don’t do that anymore. That’s the point of a tracker. You’re old school. We can follow someone out of sight now. Just like you did with the Kia.”

“Uh, sure. I realize that. I’m still having trouble getting used to the idea, though. Technology has changed the nature of the work.”

“In the end, it’s brainwork, not technology that does it. We never would have thought of going after Jasmine. The gang guys told me she broke it off with him back when he killed Mendoza eight years ago. Of course, he took off then. She never visited him in jail while he was pending trial or years before that even. Either they were doing a fantastic job of keeping the relationship under the radar, or, more likely, he just contacted her after the courtroom shooting and relighted the flame. You figured it out while geocaching by going through the drive-through wedding chapel. Amazing."

"How'd you know that? Oh." Cliff looked at the transmitter in Barry's hand. "Of course."

"Now, do we have to handcuff you, too, or are you going to return to the hotel and go home?"

"Okay, okay. I give up. Seeing Dice in cuffs is all I need. I'll leave."

At that moment a marked Sheriff's van pulled up. Cliff and Maeva watched as the FBI agents turned Dice over to the deputies from the van. The deputies produced some paperwork for the agents and Holder started to get out of the car.

Cliff seemed alarmed. "Hey, what's the deal? You're turning him over to the locals? It's a federal case now. You should be taking him in yourself, Barry. You're the case agent. You caught him. You should get the credit and the stat. You could get a raise."

"I didn't catch him. I just followed you. Besides, Nevada has the death penalty. I'm sure he'll get tried both federally and locally eventually. Chronological order doesn't matter. I have to go. Thanks to both of you. Really. That was terrific work."

Holder got out of the car, went around behind the Tesla to pull out the tracking unit, then walked over to the deputies. Maeva got out of the car, went over to the Kia and retrieved the tracker, then got back in the front seat. Cliff pulled the car away from the curb and headed back to the hotel.

"You don't have to look so smug," he said to Maeva finally.

"You're welcome. I've never liked Swiss cheese."

They checked out of the hotel and drove to the airport – Las Vegas International, not Clyburn. After they got through Security they found a restaurant and sat down to eat at the bar. There was a television playing some sporting event. Suddenly an announcer broke in with a special bulletin. She said that Van Truong, the suspect wanted in connection with the courtroom murder of two deputies, had been captured by the joint task force. "While being transported back to the jail, it is reported that he tried to escape again by grabbing a deputy's gun. He was killed by the deputies in self-defense, according to the authorities."

Chapter 26

Three Months Later
June Lake, California

"Okay, kids, go to the bathroom one last time. We're going to the snow and you won't be able to do that with your snowsuits easily," Ellen declared in her mom voice. Tommy and Mia raced each other to the bathroom. Tommy won and Mia pouted as she waited outside the hotel room bathroom.

Cliff was on the phone with Deputy Forster of the Mono County SAR team. "So everyone will be there?"

"Nearly everyone. There were some people who don't live around here who helped a lot, but they all send their congratulations and hope you and your kids enjoy the slopes. Are you about ready to leave?"

"Within five minutes or so. I really appreciate your efforts in gathering them together so I can thank everyone personally. I owe you all my life."

"That's what we do. Thanks aren't necessary, but they are always appreciated. I'm sure they'll enjoy hearing them from you almost as much as seeing you safe and sound with your family."

"Alright. I'll see you in the ski area parking lot in ten minutes or so."

"Look for the patrol car near the entrance."

"Will do."

Cliff and Ellen bundled the kids in their snow suits, packed the sleds in the car, and headed to the ski area. The parking area was only a few blocks away. The roads weren't crowded and as they pulled into the lot they could see it was almost empty. There had been little snow this early in the season and there was only one ski run open, a bunny slope covered with machine-made snow. There was a sledding area one hill for the kids, also covered with machine-made snow.

Forster waved to them as they drove in, and got in his patrol car as he waved for them to follow him. They followed his car over closer to the lodge. A line of people was forming there. Some were emerging from the lodge; others from their cars. It became clear Cliff was expected to walk the line. A few held hand-made signs welcoming him or congratulating him. The small clouds of breath confirmed the weather was in the low thirties, but it was clear and sunny.

Cliff and his family piled out of the car. Ellen told him to go ahead while she got the kids zipped up and gloved and handed them their sleds. It was his day, after all. He walked up to Forster and shook his hand, then started down the line.

Trish was first in line. She gave him a big hug and wouldn't let go until he gave her a big kiss on the forehead. Randy Whiting was next, then Darryl. Forster explained each person's role in the rescue as they walked along. Cliff spent a minute or two with every single person. When he reached the end of the line, there was a table set up with hot chocolate and doughnuts for all. Tommy and Mia ran up to the table and each grabbed a doughnut. Ellen lagged behind thanking each member for saving her husband. She received more hugs than Cliff did.

When she got to the table, Forster told them both to take out their phones and open their geocaching apps. Cliff was puzzled, but did so. The deputy told them to look for the nearest cache. When they did, they found a newly approved cache titled "Brace for Impact." The compass view pointed them toward the lodge.

"We'd like you to be FTF on this, Cliff," Forster said. "When we heard you were a geocacher, it seemed the right thing to do. The lodge was very cooperative."

"Geocaches aren't allowed to be indoors or commercial," he protested.

"It's not. It's legit."

Cliff followed the arrow towards the lodge, with Ellen following close behind. One of the SAR volunteers helped Tommy and Mia get cups of hot chocolate.

When he came to the wall of the lodge there was a large button built into the wall. Under it was mounted a small sign reading "Brace for Impact." Above the button was what appeared to be a trap door. Cliff examined it warily. If you pushed the button would something pop out and hit you? If so, what? The door was big enough to accommodate a boxing glove. Surely that wouldn't be allowed. Still, this seemed to be a pretty rough-and-tumble bunch and this was a special cache. In the end, there was nothing for it but to push the button and find out.

He stood in front of the button and lifted his hand. A murmur of anticipation rose from the small crowd behind him. Some people were shaking their heads. One was plugging his ears. Most were grinning. Ellen was making subtle motions with her head for him to move left. He decided not to take a chance. He took one step to the left since the right side was blocked by a wooden ramp and railing. Now he was out of the direct path of whatever was coming out of the trap door. He pressed the button.

Whap! He felt the impact. "What the hell!" He felt his head with his hand.

"Daddy said a bad word," Tommy announced triumphantly. Ellen was laughing hard enough to split a gut.

Cliff stepped back and realized what had happened. A toy airplane made of some sort of foam material had dropped from the eaves and hit him squarely on the head. It dangled six feet in the air. Ellen had maneuvered him expertly to the right spot. He saw the log sheet in a small, clear plastic capsule in the cockpit. The trap door was fake, a diversion. He took the capsule and extracted the log sheet. Forster handed him a pen. In the first spot where it said First To Find he wrote the date and his geocaching name, CliffNotes.

"We had to ask Ellen exactly how tall you were so we could be sure it would make contact." Forster explained. "We're going to shorten the string now so it only comes down to seven feet for future geocachers."

Ellen was still laughing, but she reached for the log sheet and took the pen. She wrote her geocaching name, Ellenwheelz, directly under his.

Cliff turned to Tommy and Mia. "Okay, kids, let's go sledding."

Acknowledgments

I owe the geocaching community so much for so many years of enjoyment. Thank you all for providing the grist for my mill. The geocaches and geocaching experiences in my novels are all either real or inspired by real caches or adventures I've heard or read about from others.

My faithful beta readers/proofreaders Jeff and Bonnie Little have yet again earned my deep and lasting appreciation, and they have it.

Not all my readers are geocachers. I hope I have provided you with a measure of entertainment even if you don't have a special appreciation for geocaching. I appreciate you for giving me an audience. Please check out my website if you want to see more Cliff Knowles novels or sign up for my mailing list. Here's the URL:

https://cliffknowles.ackgame.com/

This is a work of fiction. None of the events depicted are real, nor are any of the characters. Some of the techniques and procedures of the FBI and local law enforcement are based on my twenty-six years of FBI experience, but I retired many years ago and I'm doubtlessly out of date with FBI jargon and procedures. The reader should not take my stories, meant only to entertain, as telling the story of the real FBI.

Lastly, I must again express my gratitude to my family for their patience and the encouragement given to me for my writing. You know who you are and that I love you.

Made in the USA
Coppell, TX
30 August 2022